The Mafia's Seamstress

THE MAFIA HEIRESS SERIES

ISABEL CATRINA

Published by Isabel Catrina

Copyright © 2024 Isabel Catrina

All Right Reserved

Paperback ISBN: 979-8-9902878-0-8

Genre: Mafia romance

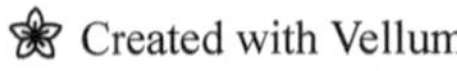 Created with Vellum

Contents

Author's Note

There is a reason this story is labeled dark-ish. Some elements take on the mafia dark romance book world but it is just a taste. This book is the beginning; not just of the series but the beginning of Lucia discovering a world she had no idea about. However she's ready to take it over.

Also don't ignore Luca just because he's blonde. He may be a blonde but he is hot…and so is Dante…and Lucia. Everyone is hot. So enjoy them because they are having a great time even though certain people are trying to steal what's theirs.

Anyway, mature audiences only. Everything sexy is done with consent between adult parties. Especially things involving slapping, degradation and praise.

Yes, this is from those TikTok videos I did.
I finally wrote it. So be good for me and read it.

Things To Know

This is an **open door romance** book so there are **adult scenes.**

<u>Trigger Warnings:</u> Death of parents and grandmother mentioned. Murder mentioned. Robbery.

<u>Spicy chapters:</u>

 6, 9, 10, 11, 15

<u>Playlist:</u>

Translations

There's a lot of Portuguese words and some Italian so here is a glossary:

1. *Avô* - Grandfather
2. Avó - Grandmother
3. *Bom dia* - Good morning
4. *Querida* - Dear
5. *Senhora* - Lady
6. *Sim (Sì in Italian)* - Yes
7. *Claro* - Of course
8. *Vai se bem* - it'll be okay
9. *Rissios* - Our version of empanadas
10. *Rissois de Galinha* - Basically chicken empanadas
11. *Tchau* - Bye
12. *Beijinhos* - Kisses (but like in a cute way)
13. *Carne guisada* - Beef stew
14. *Cozinha* - Kitchen
15. *Bolacha Maria* - Portuguese custard dessert
16. *Nos seus sonhos* - In your dreams
17. *Ora (Italian)* - Now
18. *Bella (in Italian)* - Beautiful
19. *Amore (in Italian)* - Love

20. *Beija-me* - Kiss me

21. *Gattina (in Italian)* - Little kitten

22. *Tambem* - Okay

23. *Meu amor* - My love

24. *Coelhinha* - Little rabbit

25. *Loba* - Wolf (feminine)

26. *Donna (in Italian)* - Lady Boss aka Queen

27. *Don (in Italian)* - Boss

28. *Pastei de natas* - Portuguese egg custards

29. *Você é uma* - You are a

30. *Linguiça* - Portuguese sausage

31. *Folar* - Portuguese bread with bacon and sausage

32. *Festas* - parties

33. *Eu sinto muito* - I'm very sorry

34. *Minha vida* - My life

CHAPTER 1

Family Secrets

NEVER TRUST A GOOD LOOKING FACE IN AN EXPENSIVE SUIT IF THEIR CLOTHES COST MORE THAN YOUR RENT THEN THEY'RE A WALKING RED FLAG

Dead leaves and cold breezes were wrapped around me like a scarf. The sun had fully risen and was humorously shining down on our poor freezing souls. People strolled by with quick steps as they clutched their coffee on the way to work. The sweet smell of cinnamon hung around loosely as I walked into *Maria's Padaria*.

"*Bom dia querida!*" *Senhora* Maria said from behind the counter. *Senhora* Maria was like a grandmother, an *avó* to me. Short with gray curly hair and warm brown eyes, she made the best *pastei de natas* in Loba Vista.

"*Bom dia Senhora Maria*," I said, smiling back. My eyes wandered over the sweet treats and breads I grew up on.

"*Sehnor Silva* is on a work trip, no?" she asked, already preparing my coffee.

"*Sim*. I get to be in charge," I said, eyeing the *rissios*. I smiled inwardly.

My *avô* was on a business trip. He was currently in London creating an evening wardrobe for a very special family; a family I wasn't allowed to say. He would be staying some time there since the special client was getting married. His clientele has always ranged from the elite to blue collar workers.

For him, everyone should have that feeling of being wrapped in luxury no matter their bank account. I always admire his ability to charm everyone and make them feel special.

Senhora Maria raised an eyebrow in surprise as she handed me a steaming cup of coffee. I took a sip, eyes closing. Light and sweet. Perfection.

"Will you be okay?" she asked, concerned. I fought the urge to roll my eyes because if I did it would spread like wildfire about me having a non-existing attitude.

"*Claro. Vai se bem.* I've done this before," I pointed out. *Senhora* Maria pursed her lips. She leaned to grab me some *rissois de galinha* and started making me my ham and cheese sandwich.

She was quiet. I watched her carefully. I had been left alone with the shop before. Sure it was for weekends only but still. What difference did it make if my *avô* was going to be gone for a few weeks versus two to three days. Her eyes skirted to the window where people were walking by.

"I'll be okay," I said, leaning forward. I gave her a smile to reassure her. She sighed and nodded her head. I reached for my food.

"Yes, yes. But if anyone gives you problems I send my boys," she said with a frown. I couldn't stop the giggle that tumbled out of my mouth. *Senhora* Maria's grandsons were Rafael and Mateus. They were just a few years older than me and owned the local boxing gym.

"*Senhora* Maria," I began to say. She waved her hand, cutting me off.

"I'm serious," she said, her eyes hardening. I swallowed. Growing up *Senhora* Maria was sweet and flirty. But this look? This was the look of a woman who was desperately worried. As if something horrible would happen to me.

Which was ridiculous considering the fact I knew everyone in this city. From who ran the laundromat to the grocery store. I knew my city and its people. I squared my shoulders.

"I promise. And your dress is almost done," I said. She nodded and began setting up some sweet treats. I quickly slipped what I owed in her tip jar before heading to the door.

"Ah Lucia! I told you to stop that!" she called out from behind the corner.

"And I told you to stop giving me things for free," I said with a smile. "*Tchau!*"

WALKING to work an unsettling feeling began weighing me down. My *avô* almost didn't leave for his trip because he didn't want to leave me alone with the shop. Despite the fact I had dreamt of a day like this happening. He also reminded me to go to Rafael and Mateus if anything were to happen. I snorted, taking a bite of my sandwich. I bit back a moan. Butter, bread, gooey cheese and ham. Just what I needed.

Two men in suits were crossing the street. They were black tailored suits. The corner of my lips tilted up. The lapel of their suit jacket was a dark paisley pattern. Their eyes met mine and they tilted their heads. I fought back a shiver and nodded politely.

They had come to my *avô* shop last month for suits. My *avô* sent me on an errand when they came in but I still remembered them. Both tall, dark hair and eyes. The air around them felt cold and their eyes? Eerily watchful. Like they were anticipating someone or something was going to pop out from the corners. Maybe there would be a reason to contact Rafael and Mateus.

A burgundy awning caught my eye. I smiled and excitement coursed through my body. My *avô's* shop was a dark gray building, nestled between a Portuguese restaurant and a doctor's office. It had a big window, looking into the shop and in gold vinyl it read: Silva's Seamstress Shop.

I stepped into the shop and a chill wrapped around me. Autumn was in full swing and the concrete building felt cooler inside. Switching on the lights the room was filled with racks of clothes, shoes and accessories on display.

Towards the back by the dressing room, my favorite sewing machine was waiting for me. It was begging to be threaded; to run stitches across fabrics of silk and satin. My fingers itched to feel all the different fabrics we had in stock and see what I could create.

Shrugging off my coat I made my way towards the cash register. I couldn't begin to touch my sewing machine until I double checked the calendar and turned on the register. We had a few pickups and appointments today. Nothing too hectic which meant I had time to work on orders. I needed to finish *Senhora* Maria's dress for her great nephew's baptism this weekend.

Once everything was ready I sat at my sewing machine and called my *avô*. His heavy accent croaked through the phone and a wave of warmth washed over me.

"*Bom dia querida,*" he said. I smiled at the endearment.

"*Bom dia!* Did you land okay?" I asked. I had been nervous about my *avô* flying over six hours on a plane. Naturally he grunted.

"*Sim* but I no sleep." I could hear him pacing around his hotel room.

"*Senhora* Maria's evening dress is the blue sparkle one right?" I asked despite knowing the answer. I could practically hear his eyes roll. I was a woman who liked validation, I couldn't help it.

"*Sim.* It just needs a few tucks here and there. Ah...Lucia?" I tiled my head at the sound of his hesitation.

"*Avô?*" I questioned, looking away from my to do list. It was never good when he used my actual name. He sounded unsure and my *avô* was not that kind of man. He was confident and stubborn.

"There will be a few customers coming while I'm away," he said. I chuckled.

"*Claro,*" I said, matter of factly. He let out a small cough before continuing.

"Some of them might...remember, *você é uma Silva,*" he said. I furrowed my brow. I wasn't blind to rude or aggressive customers. I used to work in retail. I remembered my days of working holidays at Always 21. He had seen my battles with impolite customers. But this felt like something else. My skin prickled and for some reason my mind went back to the two men I saw on the street.

"Of course," I responded firmly.

"I go nap, okay? The plane had me hurting. *Beijinhos*," he said, sighing in relief.

"*Beijinhos*." I stared at my phone for a moment. That was strange. But I was a Silva and therefore could handle anything. Cracking my fingers and ignoring the weird feeling running through me I got started with my day.

IT WAS a busy day with customers picking up orders, requesting pieces and measurements. I spent my entire life inside this shop. I knew where everything was like the back of my hand. It was because of my *avô* that I had a love for creating clothes.

I had an internship with a local designer after graduating but then he called needing help with his shop and I couldn't resist. I always dreamt of working side by side with him but he insisted that I get my degree first. So I did get one but in fashion design.

And now while he was away I had the shop all to myself. I breathed in deeply. This is what I've waited for. I've been waiting for him to trust me with his precious treasure that he worked so hard to get off the ground.

Silva's Seamstress Shop was the only seamstress shop in this particular area of Raven Hill County. Raven Hill County was nestled in the northeast with six cities. Loba Vista, Hare Ridge, Tiger Bay, Eagle Pointe, Wolf Grove and Hummingbird Heights.

I grew up in Loba Vista. It was a quiet town with a big Portuguese community. That was something I was heavily grateful for. I grew up on the food, music, *festas* and people. My parents and *avó* passed away when I was young and the people in the community are who helped raise me.

With the holiday season approaching I was excited to be stabbing myself accidentally with pins and yelling at my beloved sewing machine. A part of me was nervous though. Holidays were usually a busy time of year where people needed clothes fixed and a few custom pieces for parties. We typically had two other seamstresses working with me but one was getting married and the other was recovering from surgery.

Although I felt a tad overwhelmed it felt nice to have a quiet shop. And the fact my *avô* left me alone knowing all of that spoke volumes. I had his trust and the last thing I wanted to do was fuck that up. I ran a tight schedule and while this season would probably be hectic I was ready for it.

Lost in my head I faintly heard the chime of the front door.

"Excuse me?" A deep voice called out. My hands paused. The voice scraped across my skin and I felt goosebumps rise. My heart thumped in my chest. Never had a voice elicit such a reaction from me. I moved my foot off the pedal, pausing the pants I was working on. My head popped over my machine to find the face of the voice that made my body buzz.

"Hi there!" I said, nearly tripping over the leg of my work desk as I stood up. *What a great first impression.*

Stormy gray eyes collided with mine with annoyance. He was tall. *Very tall.* And I knew it because I myself nearly reached him in height. His dark hair was gelled back, perfectly, not a strand out of place. His gaze traveled up my body slowly, like a predator. I fought back a shiver at his intense and blatant stare. His eyes hardened once they reached my face.

My *avô's* words echoed in my head. He was probably the type my *avô* warned me about. His broad shoulders tensed as he took a step forward.

"I have an appointment," he said briskly. My nose twitched at his short tone. Oh, I knew his type. He wore slim fitted black slacks with a matching suit jacket and a white button shirt. He seemed clean, very stoic. Even his charcoal pocket square was pressed and most likely made from silk that was worth sixty dollars a yard. I bit the inside of my cheek. He oozed money and power, the dangerous kind. And he was terribly handsome.

But instead of feeling nervous around him I felt quite the opposite. Something about the dark gleam in his eyes compelled me towards him.

"Ah I see-"

"With Diogo," he said, cutting me off.

"My grandfather is currently away on business," I said, calmly. He scoffed and I held on to my fake smile. I had met men like him before. He was probably a man that was used to everything being handed to him when and where he wanted it. *Great.* The last thing I wanted was a rich arrogant man disturbing my peace. Sadly for him I knew how to deal with men who acted like boys.

"Well I had a fucking appointment with him and this was the only time I could come in," he bit out.

My eyes widened. Really? Cursing? Was that even necessary when we've only spoken a few sentences? Annoyance sparked across my face. My customer service mask was cracking.

I crossed my arms, making my way towards the register. I was used to rude customers and it didn't matter how much his slacks cost, he wasn't going to get away with treating me that way. I didn't care if he was having a shitty day. My shop, my rules. Well my *avô's* shop. But I was in charge, so my rules.

"One, watch your tone. Two, I understand that you having an appointment with him and him not being here is an inconvenience. However, I am here and I can help you with what you need," I said, standing behind the register. Before he could speak I held up my hand, glancing at the calendar on the counter. "You need to have your measurements taken for a suit you ordered. Pants and a jacket. Dress shirt you'll provide. Correct?"

I met his eyes. His lips thinned. I bit back a smirk. I always enjoyed putting people in their place and this man looked like he needed a kick.

"Yes," he hissed. I offered a sweet smile.

"Then I can take your measurements," I said, my customer service voice intact again.

"Are you even qualified?" he mocked, looking me up and down. He crossed his arms and my eyes snagged on how his jacket stretched across his shoulders. The suit must have been custom made with the way it molded and shifted with his body.

"The degree on the wall behind me begs to differ." I flicked a hand behind me. His eyes glanced from the wall to me. His lips twitched.

"You'll do…and sorry for the cursing that was uncalled for. It's been an unsatisfactory day and it was wrong of me to take it out on you," he said, breezing by to the back of the store where the dressing rooms were. I rolled my eyes and dug behind the counter for my measuring tape. Well at least he had the decency to apologize.

He stood on the platform in the center and I couldn't help but marvel at him despite his attitude. As an artist I couldn't deny his body made me want to grab my needle and thread. I felt the urge to wrap him in my designs. His tan skin glowed against his white crisp shirt. He would look amazing in royal blues, deep purples and rich reds.

I shook my head and started the routine. The sooner I got this done, the sooner he could leave and I could be alone again.

Shoulder to wrist. Chest to waist. Waistline-

"Are you sure that's how it's done because usually Diogo starts-" he began. I was measuring from his hip to foot when my eyes shot up to him.

"Excuse me but are you the one with the degree or the experience?" I didn't mean to sound snappy but he irritated me. It had barely been ten minutes and I was already over him.

"Well my bad Cinderella," he teased. I rolled my eyes and wrote down his next measurement. I placed the tape near his groin, about to take his inseam.

"That is a delicate area. You might want to leave a little room," he said. Our eyes connected again. He smirked and I glanced back at the measuring tape.

"Don't think you'll need much room with the measurement I just took," I muttered standing up. He dipped his head towards me and my heart flipped abnormally. His cologne engulfed me. Was this how all rich men smelled? Sandalwood and sage. It was clouding my thoughts.

I met his steady gaze bravely. He cocked his head slowly. I felt like a fly caught in a Venus fly trap. I couldn't look away from him. He had flecks of blue and flares of green around his pupils. His fingers drummed on his side nearly mimicking my heart rate.

"What did you say?" His voice was deep, making my body tighten. My stomach twisted. What was wrong with me? I needed to stop antagonizing him. But he made it so easy with every word that came from his mouth and for some reason I found it enjoyable.

"Nothing," I said, moving away. Sitting in the chair in the corner to acquire space from this man. I copied the measurements I wrote down into my laptop. "Just a few questions," I said, hoping to keep the conversation under my control. I didn't want to say anything more that could lead to a bad review. He nodded, unrolling his sleeves.

"Color?" I asked.

"Black," he said with an obvious tone.

"Like your soul?" I muttered. There goes a good review. He chuckled, shaking his head. Okay maybe a decent review.

"Do all of your customers get this kind of attitude?" he said, arching his brow. I smiled sweetly.

"I only give back what I receive," I said without thinking. Definitely a bad review.

Something about the way his steel eyes scrutinized me just made me want to poke the wolf beneath. My *avô* did always say my attitude was going to get me in trouble one day. Was today that day? He began walking towards me and I was beginning to regret my words.

"I can't say it is not undeserving but tell me," he started, standing in front of me. "Are you not aware of who I am," he asked in slight disbelief.

"Nope and I really don't care. Do you want the inside of the jacket to be plain black?" I continued. He thought about it for a moment.

"I'm okay with a pattern as long as it's dark."

I nodded. I began mumbling about cost and materials under my breath. Three long callous fingers disrupted my view of my laptop. I looked up, glaring.

"I need it in three days," he stated plainly. My eyes widened. I stood up rapidly, my chest nearly colliding with his.

"Excuse me but my *avô* won't be back for a few weeks if you want him to be the one to make your suit," I explained. He tilted his head with a smile.

"Well don't you have a degree and experience?"

Fuck. I took a deep breath. Three days for pants and jacket? I moved towards the register, his footsteps light behind me. I could possibly do it even though I had other orders I needed to get done. It was going to eat up my time for sure. I was going to have to order dinner tonight so I could finish other orders.

He arched an eyebrow, waiting. I eyed him up and down again. I could probably charge him more for the rushed order. He could definitely afford it with the watch that was on his wrist. I reached for our order forms and a pen.

"Fine," I said, agreeing to his outrageous deadline. "D.C?" I asked, remembering the initials from the calendar. I leaned against the register, my pen poised and ready.

"Yes. It stands for Dante Costa." His voice slipped around me and I froze. My heart sank to my stomach. I stared at the blank form. *No.* He couldn't be from *that* Costa family?

He chuckled darkly and it twisted my stomach. I bit down on the inside of my cheek. I needed to concentrate on the pain to keep my hand from trembling.

His chuckle proved that it was exactly what I was thinking. *Shit.* I was so fucking screwed. Why did I give him an attitude? Why couldn't I keep my mouth shut? I mean he technically started it first so my responses were valid.

His fingers slipped a strand of hair behind my ear and he lifted my chin. I looked into his eyes. They weren't cold anymore. Instead they looked interested. The last thing I wanted was to seem interesting to a member of the Costa family.

"I think you owe me something, Cinderella." He glanced at my lips and my stomach coiled in a way I hadn't felt in a while.

A thought rushed through me. While I knew some of the familiar faces that would come in growing up I also remembered the moments where I wasn't allowed to be in the room when certain people came to the shop. My brain filtered through the hazy memories rapidly and then it clicked.

Taking a deep breath I filled out the ordered form. I offered the sweetest of smiles once again.

"Yes. Your order form," I said, ripping the paper. I placed it on his chest, pushing back slightly, hoping he would back away. But he didn't. His face stayed near mine and he kept my hand on his chest. His heart pulsed in a steady rhythm beneath my fingers unlike my own. My heart was rattling in my chest as I fought to keep my composure. I didn't want to appear weak to anyone, especially to a member of the Costa family.

"You have three days. I'll be back tomorrow for a fitting," he said.

"Well I'll make you an appointment," I said calmly. He offered a small grin and I hated how it made my stomach twist in something that should have been fear. Dante Costa knew my *avô*. He called my *avô* by his first name. Which only meant one thing.

My avô worked for the mafia.

CHAPTER 2

Blue-eyed Beauty

IT'S EASY TO FALL FOR A GUY WITH BABY BLUE EYES AND A WARM SMILE BUT BE CAREFUL, THERE MIGHT BE A LION LURKING BENEATH

This wasn't how I planned my day. I woke up knowing I was going to have coffee and food from *Senhora* Maria's. I had a plan to get work done. There were things that I needed to sew and alter.

Never did I imagine I would be uncovering a family secret today; a secret that was stained with blood. My jaw tightened and he slipped the paper inside his suit jacket. Mr. Costa straightened himself. Tall, brooding and unfairly attractive.

It was always the ridiculously hot ones, wasn't it? They hid their darkness behind perfected smiles that made you feel adored. Their eyes softened in false vulnerability to lead you to believe you were the only one that mattered. However it was impossible for Mr. Costa to mask his predatory aura. It exuded from him whether he realized it or not.

"I'll be back tomorrow at six for the fitting," he said, keeping his eyes on me. I nonchalantly made my way to the front of the shop, avoiding his eyes. He needed to leave so I could breathe. I needed a minute alone to come to terms that my whole life was cracking open. It was like my family had their own pandora box and I unknowingly unlocked it.

"We close at six," I said. He brushed by me and I tried to fight the chill that went down my spine again. This man had been here for maybe half an hour and he kept eliciting reactions out of me that I shouldn't be feeling.

"You have three days to make my suit. You will be open," he said with a cocky grin. My nostrils flared as did my temper.

"I hope you understand that means I'm charging you extra," I said, crossing my arms. He tilted his head side to side, assessing me again.

"Even if I'm one of this shop's best customers?" he asked. I bit down on the inside of my cheek. He was saying this on purpose. His eyes flickered between my eyes, hoping to catch a chip in my mask. It was obvious I was unaware of this predicament with the mafia. But I didn't want him to know just how deeply it was unraveling me. Just how deep was my *avô* in this?

"Well if you are then you have no problem with me charging extra," I said with a smile. "First you're giving me three days to sew a suit during the holiday season and now you're having me work outside of our set hours," I continued. I took a step towards him, wrapping myself in his cologne again. His pupils dilated and his shoulders tensed beneath his suit.

"Knowing who you are, I say you can afford it," I finished. Mr. Costa clicked his tongue.

"Does your grandfather know just how much of a vixen his granddaughter is?" he asked. I sucked in a breath. I had never been called a vixen before and hearing it from his lips about it made my heart pound.

"Have a lovely day," I said, holding the door open. Two men in black suits stood outside. They reminded me of the men from this morning. I wondered just how many people that I walked by on a daily basis were wolves in sheep's clothing. They glanced at me then at Mr. Costa. Mr. Costa nodded.

"Bye Cinderella," he said as he walked out. Once the door was shut and I was safely alone I sucked in a deep breath. Tears pricked my eyes as I wandered around the shop I grew up in. I loved this place. I loved my family.

And yet staring at the walls I helped decorate, everything felt like a lie. It was like the home I've known my entire life was covered in wallpaper decorated with warmth, lavender and love. But now it was ripped open to reveal a house filled with lies, broken bones and blood.

The fucking mafia. I kept repeating in my head. Everything made sense now. The secretive appointments, the amount of times I needed to stay in the back room or leave, the hush whispers behind closed doors. It all made sense now. How hadn't I noticed any of it?

My hands began to shake. My throat tightened and my stomach threatened to throw up my breakfast. How could this be? My sweet *avô* working for murderers. Did they have something on him? Was it his choice? Like a house of cards crumbling beneath a gentle breeze my life was being swept from under me.

Staring at my phone I debated on calling him. He had answers to the questions taking root in my mind. But the business trip he was on was too important. It meant spreading the Silva name across seas.

In these moments I wished I still had my parents. I wished I had some kind of family to rely on. But my only source of truth and warmth was six hours across the Atlantic. My thoughts drifted back to *Senhora* Maria. Did she know?

Taking a deep breath I reminded myself that if he's been doing this for years so could I this one time. This would be the only time. I could keep up the pretense of knowing nothing and continue on with my days.

I would make Mr. Costa his suit and that would be the end of it. I didn't need to be anymore involved then this one time and I was going to make sure my *avô* would no longer be either. Whatever agreement he had with the mafia was going to end one way or the other.

Shaking my head I got back to work. I had two pants to hem and one dress that needed extra lace before I could work on Mr. Costa's suit. It was time to do what I did best.

Swallow the pain and stress and get shit done.

THE NEXT DAY I was working with a throbbing headache. The Gomes family needed all of their kids' pants to have alterations for their cousin's baptism for the weekend. My fingers were cramping and I skipped lunch. Again.

I could hardly sleep. My brain kept replaying nightmares. I was trapped in a tower in a torn gown with nothing but a broken mattress and a sewing machine. Men in dark suits with faces hidden beneath the shadows of moonlight were threatening me to make clothes.

I woke up in a cold sweat with my heart pounding in my chest. I would rather attempt to spin straw into gold than work for the mafia but somehow my *avô* trapped us in this situation. A situation that I was purposefully left in the dark about.

A glance out the window showed people bustling, leaves falling and a cool breeze blowing. Everyone seemed at ease. They were oblivious that the mafia was walking among them. Not aware that this tiny family owned shop worked for them. My hands trembled as I tried to sew the final stitch on Ms. Gomes' son's pants.

"Miss?" An easy voice called out. I flinched. I hadn't even heard the bell chime because I was so focused. My vision focused on a tall, lean man with blonde wavy hair and blue eyes. He had an easy smile with dimples. He wore a dark blue dress shirt, tucked into gray pants.

My head tilted as I took in his clothes. Shirt was standard but the pants were molded across his legs. As he took a step inside they stretched across his thighs. They were most likely mainly polyester.

The door closed gently behind him as he walked through. He offered another smile as he made his way towards me with a model's grace. Two hot men in two days. That was definitely a record. I gave him a warm smile, the customer service mask turned on.

"Sorry! Spaced out a second. How may I help you?" I said as I made my way quickly behind the cash register to meet him.

"That's okay. Are you new?" he asked. A bubble of laughter erupted out of me. No one had ever asked me that. Everyone knew everyone or knew someone who knew everyone in Loba Vista.

"I didn't mean to laugh, sorry. This is my grandfather's shop," I said. His left eye twitched and recognition dawned on his face.

"You're Lucia?" he asked softly. I blushed at his tone. It was a mix of gentle awe and surprise. I nodded politely.

"Wow. He's always talked about you. How talented and beautiful you are. He was definitely right," he said, moving to stand directly in front of me. I had to slightly tilt my head up to meet his eyes. He looked at me warmly. I bit the inside of my cheek. Staring at the man before me I would have definitely remembered if he had been in the shop.

But if he knew my *avô* well enough to know about me. Was he one of the clients I wasn't supposed to know about? A dark feeling began crawling up my body.

"You haven't seen my talent yet, only my beauty," I pointed out. A smirk tugged on his lips before he dropped his elbows on the counter, cocking his head. Now we were eye level and I could see just how blue his eyes were. There were flecks of honey around the pupil; like a sunflower against a clear sky.

"If you work for Diogo you must be talented," he said.

"Are you flirting with me?" I asked. His gaze traveled all over my face and my heart skipped. This man was ungodly attractive.

"This is me being me," he said. I shook my head but then he leaned forward and I got a sniff of pine. Hot men who smell delicious might be a weakness I didn't realize I had. I felt trapped in his gaze.

"If I was flirting with you, you wouldn't be questioning it," he said. I blushed furiously. Fuck, he was smooth.

"So how can I help you," I said, redirecting the conversation. He leaned away and I could finally breathe.

"I'm here to pick up a suit," he said. I nodded, pulling out a notebook that held all of the orders. "It'll be under LB," he said. I nodded, finding his name and order number. I excused myself to the back to find his suit. When I returned he was eyeing the window outside.

"Mr. LB here is your suit," I said, handing it over. His chuckle was rough and it made my stomach tightened.

"LB are initials," he said, as he took the suit from me. That dark feeling was back and crawling higher. I marked his order as picked up when I felt his breath on my ear. "It stands for Luca Benanti," he whispered. Tendrils of shadows wrapped around my chest, making it harder to breathe. You have to be mother fucking kidding me.

"B-benanti?" I stuttered. He nodded. *Double fuck.* I clenched my jaw, trying to remain calm. I could not freak out on him. I could not let him see me lose my shit. I needed to be the picture of cool and collected. I had refused to let Mr. Costa see me break apart and Mr. Benanti wouldn't either.

My eyes skated to him and he smiled warmly. I recognized his last name. If I remembered the rumors right Costa and Benanti were family or at least related somehow.

"He talks about you a lot," Mr. Benanti said, pulling away. I placed the notebook under the register to hide my fidgeting hands.

"Oh god. I hope it's not embarrassing," I said, squeezing my fingers. Why the fuck was my *avô* talking to the damn mafia about me?

"Oh no, nothing of the sort. He just mentions how proud he is of you," he said. He pushed a hair behind my ear like Mr. Costa did but with Mr. Benanti, it was a different thrill that went through me. I stared at him in surprise. This man belonged to a dangerous family and yet around him I felt like I was bathing in sunlight.

Oh dear god, was it going to be like those books I read where years ago my *avô* promised me in marriage to one of them? I wasn't ready for marriage. I hadn't even been on a date in two years.

"Well I'm glad and thank you so much for doing business with us," I said, hoping he would take the hint to leave.

"It's always a *pleasure* doing business with Silva's Seamstress Shop," he said.

Always. Just how deep was my *avô's* relationship with the mafia?

The door dinged and I turned to greet the customer, grateful to get away from Mr. Benanti. But that greeting soured quickly.

"You're early," I said, glaring at Mr. Costa. I glanced at my watch. He was two hours early actually. Maybe with him already here I could close on time. He grunted, making his way over.

"I had some unexpected cancellations," Mr. Costa said. He was focused on Mr. Benanti who hadn't paid him any attention since he walked in.

"Well I'm with a customer. You can wait in the corner," I said, waving him towards a seat. Mr. Costa's jaw locked in place and he raised an eyebrow. There was a soft chuckle from the blue-eyed beauty in front of me.

"I will not sit in the corner like a child," Mr. Costa said. I fought the urge to roll my eyes.

"This attitude you walked in with resembles that of one," I said. Mr. Costa glared at me.

"Really? Because I walked in and you immediately glared at me," he said. Mr. Benanti looked between us.

"You walked into this shop and glared at my customer first," I said. Which was true. The second he stepped through this door and looked at Mr. Benanti his demeanor shifted. My statement must have sparked something because Mr. Costa's fists clenched.

"I was just leaving, cousin," Mr. Benanti said casually. Before turning away he looked at me and said softly, "I'll be seeing you around."

"Thank you for trusting us with your order *Luca*," I said, sweetly. Mr. Benanti's smile widened and he gave me a quick wink. He turned to walk away, his eyes meeting Mr. Costa's. For a moment they stared at each other until he finally left.

"What a charming smile you gave him," Mr. Costa said through gritted teeth. I went to grab the fabric to cut his suit.

"He's a paying customer," I said. He grunted again. I spread the fabric across my work table and reached for my scissors.

"Even if he's in the mafia?" he asked. I clutched the scissors in my hands and looked into Mr. Costa's eyes. A quick thought raced through me as I held onto the scissors. He peered at my hand. The corner of his lips twitched as he fought back what I assumed was a smirk.

"Well you're still here aren't you?" I fired back. There was a spark in his gaze. I needed to stop being so damn interesting. "Listen, I've been busy so I'll be cutting your suit now. You're going to have to wait before I get you to try it on," I said. He nodded in understanding. I sighed. If he could stay silent we would have no problems.

He took a seat by the shoes and pulled out his phone. I smiled to myself. He ended up in the corner just like I told him.

I CONCENTRATED on measuring the fabric and cutting out the pattern pieces. I decided to go with a black tweed fabric. It felt right given the current weather. Most people went with velvet or standard cotton.

But this suit was for a charity ball. One of the most famous ones in our city. The event was going to be crawling with the rich of the rich. A black tweed suit would make him seem sophisticated and give him the old money look that he oozed.

As for the lining I was going to hold off for now. I hadn't found the right pattern to match. Halfway through cutting my hands began to shake. The headache was pounding now. I knew I shouldn't have skipped lunch again. I felt Dante's eyes on me.

"Is everything-" before he could finish his sentence my stomach growled. His eyebrows shot up and his lips twitched. "Hungry Cinderella?" he teased. I sat back and mumbled a yeah. There was no point in denying it. He shook his head. "Didn't you eat lunch?"

Looking over at him, I stretched my arms, taking a calming breath. He was sitting in the chair, legs spread out. His thighs stretch against his navy slacks. His button up black shirt was practically painted on his chest. Definitely another custom made piece.

God, he was exquisite. The same itching feeling in my fingers came alive. But my stomach conquered the urge to sew. His full lips were twisted in a lopsided grin.

"No. I was busy," I said. His gaze hardened and he pulled out his phone.

"I'll order food. You shouldn't be skipping meals," he said.

"Obviously. But if you haven't noticed I have a lot of work including a suit that I have barely three days to put together," I said. He ignored my sassy remark and kept scrolling through his phone.

"What do you want?" he asked. Looking at him I was tempted to say something that would ensure a flirtatious response. And it was appealing enough that I couldn't stop myself from saying it.

"Anything but Italian," I said. He smirked, shaking his head. I stretched my fingers and went back to finishing cutting the fabric. I could have sworn I heard him say, for now.

CHAPTER 3

Why Are Mafia Men Hot?

IF YOU CAN'T STAND THE HEAT, GET OUT OF THE KITCHEN UNLESS…

I may have done a miscalculation. I didn't realize just how big of a distraction Mr. Costa would be. Even though he confined himself to a chair and his phone, his presence was suffocating…in the most peculiar way.

The thread slid out of the needle again. I cursed under my breath. Every few stitches my eyes wandered to the man sitting in the corner and my fingers were aching to do something that didn't involve sewing.

I grunted as I attempted to rethread the stupid needle. I pricked my finger..again. This time I didn't dare look at him. He would probably make some snide remark about my focus and whether or not the degree on the wall was in fact mine.

The door dinged open and a man in a suit carrying plastic bags walked in. The smell immediately made my stomach growl. Mr. Costa stood up and took the bags from who I assumed was his minion. I hated to admit even the minion had a decent looking suit.

I watched as they whispered under hush breaths. It must be nice to have someone on your beck and call. Someone to do your dirty work, your laundry and errands. I could use someone to do my laundry. I snorted. Mr. Costa turned to the side to look at me and I went back to my stitches. Once his minion was out the door he flipped the sign to close.

"Um, we're not close," I said.

"We're eating lunch now," he said sternly.

"At this point this would qualify as early dinner," I pointed out. He moved to stand in front of me and waved at me to stand up. I crossed my arms and sat back. He scoffed before turning to head to the back. "Where are you going?" I asked.

"I've had coffee with your grandfather plenty of times to know where the kitchen in this building is. Now get up," he said with an authoritarian tone that both heated my blood for more than one reason. He stood waiting in the hallway that led to the dressing rooms, the office and the kitchen.

"There's windows out here so if you try something I have a witness," I said, cooly, pointing to the front of the shop. A dark chuckle escaped his lips and fuck it was deep and gravely.

"You think an audience would stop the *Don* of the Italian mafia?" he said, voice dipping. My face flamed as thoughts raced through my head. Thoughts I only had when I was curled up in bed with a book. Ignoring his comment and the way his tone affected me I stood and followed him towards the back room.

It was a small kitchen. A table, four chairs, sink, some cabinets, microwave and a small fridge. I eyed our coffee machine.

I've had coffee with your grandfather plenty of times to know where the kitchen in this building is.

I needed to know just how deep my *avô* was with the mafia. The man before me held all the answers. When did this start? How did it start? And most importantly how do I end it?

I sat across from Mr. Costa as he set the bags on the table and began taking out the food. I needed to ask questions in a way that didn't make the wolf in front of me feel cornered. A whiff of tomato and oregano crossed my nose.

"I thought I said no Italian," I said, breaking the silence. My voice came out harsher than intended but he seemed to brush it off.

Casting a sideways glance he said, "I know. This is for me."

Opening the second bag the smell reminded me of home; garlic, wine and red peppers. My stomach growled again.

"Is that-" Before I could finish Mr. Costa smirked.

"This is your grandpa's favorite. Figured you would like it," he said. He walked over and set the takeout container in front of me. It was the good kind. One I could easily reuse at home. I tilted my head back to stare into his gray eyes. A strand of black hair fell forward and I was tempted to brush it back.

"Your food," he said, his voice husky.

"Thank you Mr. Costa," I said, keeping his gaze. The side of his mouth twitched.

"Mr. Costa uh?" he said it as if it was funny. He finally walked away and I greedily grabbed the container. The delicious beef stew was still hot. The smell made my mouth water. I haven't had a proper meal all day.

"*Carne guisada* goes really well with ri-" he held up a carton of rice, cutting me off. I fought back a smile and he came back to my side with the side dish.

"I know," he said.

MEMORIES OF SUNDAY lunch with the family floated around as we ate in silence. My mom and *avó* would be in the kitchen while my *avô* and dad were outside grilling and watching a soccer game. I faintly remember other people from the Portuguese community being there.

My *avós* house was *the* house for the community. Everyone was always coming over to hang out and eat food. I felt a prickle in the back of my head. Things changed drastically when my parents and my *avó* died. I had lost them around the same time.

After that things changed and the community fell apart. Now while we walked around giving pleasantries to each other there was distance. Even with *Senhora* Maria it was as if there was something hanging between us. I stared at my food. It tasted so much of the home I used to have and forgot about.

"Did you get this from *Duarte's Cozinha*?" I asked. He nodded quietly, taking a bite of pasta. My brain rummaged through my childhood memories. *Duarte's Cozinha* had always been one of the only Portuguese restaurants in Loba Vista that offered breakfast, lunch and dinner. And now it is being run by Duarte Jr.

"Dj was always a great cook. Took after his grandpa," I said, taking a bite. "I'm happy he's keeping it going," I said, swallowing hard.

"It's always good to see the kids take on the tradition and keep it alive," Mr. Costa said. My stomach tightened. One day this shop would mine. Something I always wanted to keep going. But my problem now was the mafia.

"Thank you," I said quietly after a bit. Mr. Costa leaned back in surprise as he wiped his lips.

"I believe that's the first nice thing you've said to me, Cinderella," he said.

"I'm ready to take it back," I said, blankly.

"But then you wouldn't have dessert," he said as pulled a small container from the bag. I raised an eyebrow.

"Depends on the dessert," I said, crossing my arms. His lips formed a smirk I was becoming addicted to. He opened it, revealing one of my favorite Portuguese desserts.

"Is that *bolacha maria*?!" I said in shock. I hadn't had it in a long time. It was a layered cake of egg custard, cookies dipped in espresso and whip cream topped with cinnamon.

"Say thank you again and it's yours," he teased. I looked at him and then the dessert.

"You should give me dessert seeing how I have to work overtime to make your suit," I pointed out. He looked at me for a second before sliding the cake over to me. "Smart choice Mr. Costa," I said with a smirk.

My mouth watered as I dug a spoon into its creamy deliciousness. A groan escaped my lips and I felt Mr. Costa's stare. My mouth exploded in flavors of sugar, cinnamon and coffee. He shifted in his seat and muttered something in Italian.

My brain began to attempt to translate. I didn't speak Italian but I spoke Spanish and Portuguese. Once you knew one romance language it wasn't hard to figure out the others. If I got it right I think he said, *that noise will get you in trouble.*

My cheeks flushed. The familiar feeling from before began spreading. He said that from hearing me moan about the cake which was in fact moan worthy. He, however, was not. At least that's what I kept trying to convince myself. But it was hard when he looked the way he did and made me feel things I knew I shouldn't be feeling.

"Nos seus sonhos," I said in Portuguese and from the look in his eyes I had translated his Italian correctly. His gray gaze heated for a second. A slow smirk stretched across his face.

"Oh they will be Cinderella," he said in English. I scoffed at him.

"No they won't," I retorted.

"And who are you to tell me what to do while I'm dreaming?" he asked, leaning on the table. Fuck. There I went, being interesting again. But Mr. Costa felt like burning fire and his flames enticed me.

"Lucia Silva," I said, shrugging my shoulders nonchalantly. I was well aware this man could snap my neck in half but for some reason I wanted to see how far I could push him.

"I don't like your attitude," he said as his nostrils flared.

"One, I don't care. Two, you don't need to since I'm just a commoner making your suit. And three, I can't stand your high and mighty attitude and therefore will continue to put you in your place," I said. His fists clenched. Okay, maybe I pushed him too far.

"No one puts me in my place," he spat out. I chuckled.

"Last time I checked I had you sitting in a corner," I recounted, keeping my eyes on him. Men like Mr. Costa expected people to flinch under his gaze, crack under his words and break beneath his hands. But that was not and would never be me. I didn't look away. I wouldn't give him the satisfaction of thinking he intimidated me.

My body began feeling hot as his eyes traveled down my face in what looked like appreciation. I bet he wasn't used to someone going toe to toe with him. I bet no one ever challenged him.

Until me.

The thought excited me. I was a Silva and I was raised to fight and stand my ground. The thought of bringing a man like Mr. Costa to his knees was seductive.

"Put the food down," he commanded. His words crawled up my skin, sending goosebumps everywhere. My heart pounded against my chest.

Was this the voice of a *Don*? His aura shifted to something darker. Instead of scaring me it called to me. The darker side of his voice was alluring. I wanted more. So I ignored his command. I was intrigued to see what he would do if I didn't.

I leaned against my chair further, taking another spoonful of cake. I closed my eyes, savoring the taste. I faintly heard his chair screeched against the tile floor. When I opened my eyes he began stalking his way towards me. My breathing faltered for a second. The wolf had come out to play. My heart rattled against my chest.

"Stand," he said through clenched teeth. Once again I didn't. "*Ora*," he said.

I bit my tongue. His Italian was tempting and it did just enough to get me to obey. I set my cake down and slowly rose. I was at eye level with his lips and I let my gaze unfocus. I didn't need my eyes showing him how he was affecting me. He leaned in. Soft lips brushed my ear and I dug my nails into my palms, fighting back a shiver. His heat was engulfing me, his cologne smothering me.

"Make no mistake that I allow you to be bold. The only reason I haven't snuffed out that little fire you have brewing is because of your grandfather," he said, gripping my chin with his hand. I was forced to stare into his steel gaze. I breathed in sharply at the skin to skin contact. "If that wasn't the case you would have already been on your knees begging for forgiveness," he said. I hated the way my body responded to his statement. I yanked my face away from his hand.

"Begging for forgiveness for speaking the truth? Never. On my knees? When the mood strikes," I said. We stayed staring at each other in a silent battle. For a second I thought he was going to say something, do something by the way his hands kept flexing but then he turned away.

"We need to finish eating so you can work on my suit. We don't have all day," he said. I sneered as the wolf retreated back to his corner. I continued to eat my cake and remind myself that he was a temptation that I couldn't afford. He was a part of the fucking mafia for crying out loud.

THE LATE EVENING turned into night as I made sure to make a to do list of all the things needed to get done and by when. Mr. Costa's suit at the moment was top priority due to the deadline but I didn't want to fall behind on my other customers. While sewing the baste stitch on his pants I decided to bring up Mr. Benanti.

"Question. How exactly do you and Luca know each other?" I asked. I heard a sharp intake of breath. I made sure to innocently look up at him. I wanted to know more about their relationship and connection to my *avô*. His fingers were paused on his cell.

"We're family," he said, watching me.

"Really?" I asked. Those two were complete opposites. Light and dark and not just with features.

"Sadly," he said as he stretched his legs. After a few more stitches I couldn't resist asking more questions.

"Why do you not like him?" I asked.

"He's a pain in my ass and always around," he said simply.

"He doesn't seem like bad company," I commented. While being around Mr. Costa made me feel like every single one of my nerves were on fire, being around Luca for a few minutes calmed the storm within.

"Because of our status we're always together and the fucker likes to talk," he said, stretching his arms. Once again I was enamored by the way his shirt seemed to stretch with his muscles. Where the fuck did he buy his shirts? Did someone make them? Can they teach me?

"Oh I get that. I read about that in a mafia romance book," I said. My hands froze. Fucking shit. Mr. Costa's eyes bore into mine. His mouth set in amusement.

"What have you read?" he asked. He was intrigued...again. I sewed three stitches before I regained my composure.

"I've read some books," I said. I hoped my tone sounded nonchalant, borderline bored.

"Please continue. I'd love to know what happens in these books," he said. I rolled my eyes.

"I need to sew," I said. He chuckled. It was deep and intoxicating. I was slowly, in a short time of 24 hours becoming addicted to it. I seriously need to get laid. I could *not* be attracted to a chuckle that came out of a man that beat up people for a living. He's probably killed someone with his bare hands. Those big, calloused bare hands that would feel great against my bre-

"Fine. But I'm going to bring this up again at some point," he said with a wolfish grin. I bet that was the grin that got him away with plenty of things. Maybe that was the same grin that tricked my family into working with the mafia. But something deep down told me that that was wrong. There was something I was missing.

SOME TIME HAD PASSED and the baste stitching was done. I sat back, rolling my shoulders.

"What kind of stitch is that?" he asked, walking back to me.

"It's a baste stitch. Essentially the stitch is really long so that when you try it on if it's too big or tight I can pull out the string easily without damaging the fabric and sew again," I said. "I needed to give my machine a break so I did the last bit of it by hand."

"That makes sense," he said, nodding at the fabric. I fought back a smile. This was the first time someone had seemed to take genuine interest in what I did. I stared at the garment in my hands. It was a talent to take something and transform it. It's why I loved sewing. When it came to fabrics there was endless creativity and possibilities. I nodded, standing up with the pants.

"Is this the part where I strip?" he asked. I grabbed my pincushion and made my way to the dressing rooms.

"This is the part where I try not to stab you," I said over my shoulder. He chuckled, following behind me.

Once in the back of the shop Mr. Costa slipped behind the curtain. There was a tiny stage that was surrounded by three mirrors and about four dressing rooms. I secured the pincushion to my wrist before walking to hand Mr. Costa the pants.

"Here's the pants," I said in front of his dressing room. The curtain abruptly opened revealing Mr. Costa in his black boxer briefs. His legs were long, thick and muscular like a soccer player. My weakness.

He had a black lines that swirled around from his ankle, up his left leg that slipped underneath his briefs and reappeared to crawl up to his left pec. My gaze eventually made its way to his face. He truly was handsome. Without a word of acknowledging my blatantly staring he gave me a lopsided grin as I handed him his pants.

"You didn't need to take off your shirt," I pointed out.

"Can't concentrate?" he teased. I rolled my eyes, turning away from him. There was a bit of rustling behind me.

I stood in front of the stage and watched Mr. Costa take center. I held my breath. Not because he was going to be wearing something that I designed but because I always got anxious during this part.

If my measurements were too big that was an easy fix. But if it was too small and there wasn't enough space I would have to recut the fabric all over again and that would be a pain in the ass. The fabric glided up his legs and laid slightly loose at his hips.

I sat back on my heels, staring at where the fabric sat on him. It could be tighter in certain places, specifically the inside of his thighs. My focus shifted gears to work mode as I began pinning. I made my way down his legs before going back to his thighs. I checked the way the pants shaped across his muscles.

While I wanted it to fit in certain places I also wanted the fabric to move with him. There was a tap on the top of my head. I glared at Mr. Costa. His eyes were like melted silver.

"See. I told you, you would be on your knees," he said.

"Please remember I'm holding pins," I said deadpan. His eyes sparkled with mischief. My hands made their way to tighten his waistline.

Right now they sat slightly too loose at his hips. My eyes wandered to his toned stomach and the way the waves of his tattoo. He had scars. Some were tiny scratches, some red and raised and some jagged. I swallowed. These were the markings of a man whose life revolved around fighting and surviving.

"So about those mafia romances?" His question interrupted my thoughts causing me to slip a pin into his hip. I gasped although he didn't flinch. I immediately looked at him.

"I'm sorry!" I exclaimed. He chuckled.

"A little pain never hurts," he said softly. My cheeks warmed. I bit the inside of my bottom lip as certain scenes began filtering through my head. He was right. A little pain never hurts, not when done in a delicious way. A safe, delicious way of course.

"I told you we wouldn't be talking about that," I said. I checked the other side of his hip and glanced down. *The ankle is a bit wide on this side.*

"I mean I can't tell you if what you read is true but there's a few things I could show you," he said. My stomach dropped.

"What do you mean show?" I asked, my eyes fixated on his right ankle. He hummed softly. He was going to drive me insane. He was a walking temptation.

I shook my head, backing away from him. The left calf needed to be taken in as well. Other than that it didn't look too bad. I stood up and he lifted my wrist that had the pincushion wrapped around it. His fingers moved softly across until he found the end of a pin. His eyes flickered up.

The air around us began spinning, pushing and pulling until my chest brushed his. His warmth cocooned me. His tongue darted out to lick his bottom lip and I couldn't stop myself from watching. My eyes went back to his finger. He pressed against the thin metal and I gasped as a bead of blood formed.

"If you read mafia romances then you know that there is an overlap between pain and pleasure," he began. My heart banged against my chest and my thighs clenched. He brought his finger to his lips and licked it clean. "And like I said, a little pain never hurts."

A phone blared from the dressing room slicing through our tension. I waved him off, needing to get myself under control. My face and frankly my whole body was boiling.

Of course I thought about those things. I've read about women getting tied up, slapped across the ass and ears filled with filthy words that make them pant. Those things intrigued me. But I wasn't sure if that was something I was into. I glanced at Mr. Costa. I wondered if he could show me.

"Shipment..tonight…" My ear kept picking up bits and pieces from his phone call bringing me back to reality.

All of a sudden I was reminded of what Mr. Costa was, of whom my *avô* really worked for. It was one thing to be around him but to actually hear parts of a life I only read in books and seen on tv was another thing. Now it felt too real.

I had so many questions but maybe I wasn't ready to face them yet. I chewed my bottom lip coming to the conclusion I would rather live in my bubble for one more night. With shaky hands I grabbed the pants from Mr. Costa as he came out from the dressing room. He stared at me with worried filled eyes.

"Nothing has ever happened to your grandfather in this shop. It's safe," he assured me. I didn't ask for this confession but I felt relief in it. I still wondered how long this twisted relationship my *avô* was in has gone. Would I have to carry it on? Taking a deep breath I gave him a hard look.

"That may be the case for *him*. But one day this will be my shop. And if history has taught us anything it has taught us that men will use women to get to other men," I said and began walking towards the front of the shop. "You can't assure me that when this place is mine that my safety or this shop won't be used as a pawn," I said over my shoulder.

I packed his pants in my bag, planning to continue sewing it at home. Mr. Costa passed me on the way to the front door. His hand hovered over the doorknob while his gray gaze rooted me to the ground.

"That's true Ms. Silva. But are you a pawn?"

TODAY THERE WERE no appointments and the shop was peaceful. I sewed, stitched and cut fabric to distract myself. It was another sleepless night of my head being consumed with questions. Why my *avô*? How did he get mixed in this? How much were my parents involved? Why did no one tell me? I wanted to call my *avô* but I knew he was too busy in England.

Before I knew it, Mr. Costa's pants and Amalia's dress for the upcoming charity were finished. My hands were killing me and the headache from yesterday was still hanging around in the outskirts of my brain. Putting everything away I gritted my teeth.

A dull ache that began on the left side of my head was spreading. Yesterday I ignored the headache but another one today was a signal of something else coming. But I didn't want to think about it. I took a deep breath, gathering my things. It was late afternoon and soon Mr. Costa would be here for his appointment. I just needed to go over inventory, have him try on the clothes and then go home.

The bell above the door rang. Turning around it was Luca. His blonde hair was gelled back. He wore a gray suit that made his blue eyes stand out.

"What are you doing here?" I asked. My stomach tightened. Hopefully it was something clothing related and nothing else. I really didn't need this right now. He placed his hands in his pockets.

"I did say I'll see you around," he said with a grin. I rolled my eyes.

"I didn't think '*around*' meant the next day. We must have different definitions," I said looking back at my inventory list. We needed more black satin, threads and needles.

"What can I say? I couldn't get your sweet smile out of my head," he said with a grin. While Mr. Costa was brooding and dark but Luca was the sun, pulling everyone into his gravity.

"What do you need?" I said asking in my customer service voice. Luca's eyes glanced around the shop and I lowered my hand beneath the counter. We had an emergency button that alerted the cops.

While I hoped I didn't need to use it I watched Luca's eyes travel to the corners of the shop. I inwardly cursed. We were supposed to install cameras during the summer but we started getting orders for the fall festivities and that plan was forgotten.

"Need? What if I simply needed your presence?" he asked. I scoffed.

"Mr. Benanti, we had a five minute conversation. Don't tell me it only took a few sentences from a beautiful face to win you over," I said. Luca walked over to the register and my finger touched the side of the alarm button.

"I'd prefer if you would call me Luca. Mr. Benanti is *so* formal," he said. I rubbed the alarm button once. His eyes remained trained on me but he rested a hand on the counter, his fingers drumming.

"It's formal because of the status of our relationship," I said simply.

"And how do I change that?" he asked. A giggle escaped me before I could stop it. I've heard stories about the mafia my whole life. Hell, I read mafia romance books. With everything I've read and heard about the mafia, Mr. Costa completed the description. But Luca? He seemed to be the opposite. Did this golden retriever of a man have a bite? Or was he all bark?

"I don't like mixing business with pleasure. Now tell me, is there anything you need from Silva's Seamstress Shop?" I asked. My hand fell away from the button and I began updating the inventory list I had on a spreadsheet. Luca leaned away from the counter, taking his hand away.

"Dante told me to come by and hang until he got here," he said. I snorted.

"I don't need a babysitter from men I hardly know," I said. "Even if they're friends with my *avô*," I added.

"He sent me to watch a beautiful woman. Can't say I'm mad about it," he said with a shrug of his shoulders. I narrowed my eyes at the blonde beauty.

"I'm not getting in between you and your cousin," I said, typing on my laptop. The dull ache was coming back harder. I could feel its tendrils spreading across the left side of my head. I took deep breaths through my nose.

"Why not? That sounds like a nice position," he said. My stomach clenched. I looked up at him, assessing. He had an easygoing smile and the look in his eyes promised delicious mischief. Luca was just as tempting as Mr. Costa.

"Who says I want to be in any sort of position with you and Mr. Costa?" I asked, titling my head up in defiance towards him. Luca leaned against the counter and I was again smothered in his cologne. Dear God, did all mafia men smell this delicious? His scent was a mixture of citrus, cardamom and cedar this time.

"Your blushing face says otherwise," he said with a crooked grin. My eyes snapped back towards my laptop and I waved him away.

"Just sit in the corner and stay quiet," I demanded.

"Don't worry, I'll be enjoying the view," he said, walking towards the door. With a wink he flipped the sign close and sat down.

IF MR. COSTA was a distraction Luca was right there with him. I felt his gaze crawling all over me, reading me. But I knew Luca wouldn't sit still. During our whole conversation he kept fidgeting with his hands and slightly rocking on his feet when he stood. It was as if he was anticipating something happening and waiting. He walked around the store staring, feeling fabrics. I enjoyed the quiet for about another hour and a half until he came up to the cash register, standing in front of me.

"So I guess now you know," he said softly. My heart lurched and I did my best to keep my face neutral. I hadn't outright spoken to anyone about the whole mafia thing.

With Mr. Costa we were always bickering and I didn't want to interrupt my *avô* on his trip. However I couldn't help but feel like I was missing a piece of the truth. I nodded.

"How are you holding up?" he asked. The corner of my lips twitched. That was sweet of him to ask. Taking a deep breath, I stretched my back. His ocean blue eyes had one clear emotion, concern.

"Honestly? Terrified. Confused. Angry. Relief?" I said, trying to describe what I was feeling. He looked taken aback by the word relief. "Well it kind of helped my childhood make more sense. I remember so many moments of being hushed out of a room or taken for a walk while some clients came in," I explained. I began darting my eyes back and forth as if looking for the missing pieces of my childhood. Because there was something I was still missing.

"Little things that even though I never paid attention to never made sense and now they do," I said. He nodded in approval. I closed my laptop and moved to grab Mr. Costa's suit jacket. I needed him to try it so I could finalize the stitching.

"It's a good thing that you know about the mafias now," Luca said casually. I froze mid-step.

"Plural?" I asked, my stomach dropping. I was going to be sick. A smirk graced his pretty face.

"I guess there's still some things you don't know. Wolf Grove, that's us. Hare Ridge, that's the Irish. Your friend Danny works for them. Tiger Bay are the Koreans. Although they're leaving the area to someone else. A different family from overseas. The main family is retiring, rightfully so. Hummingbird Heights are the Jamaicans. And Eagle Pointe are the Americans," he explained. "They think they're the shit. They're not," he sneered.

I was completely surrounded by murderous people. I bit the inside of my cheek. Danny was a part of the mafia? Daniel Callahan was a doctor. He was always the brightest in class. How many more of the people I grew up with were involved without my knowledge?

"Danny is a doctor!" I said. Luca nodded.

"Someone needs to pull out the bullets and sew up the holes," he said. "But don't worry! Your gramps shop is on neutral ground. Everyone agrees to leave this area alone. Everyone needs a suit and he's the best in town," he rushed out.

So I was right. This area was uncontrolled by no one. But why didn't that feel right? Neutral ground simply because of clothes? There had to be more to this story.

I eyed the notebook under the cashier that had the client list. *Just how many of them?* I placed Mr. Costa's jacket on my work table. I faintly heard Luca's footsteps behind me.

"So I would be careful who you throw that pretty smile to," he said.

Luca grinned at me and heat coursed through me. For a man who could probably kill with his bare hands he had a pretty face.

"Are you including yourself in that?" I questioned, leaning against the table.

"I'm number two on the list of men you need to watch out for." His voice was rough. I felt myself leaning in, being pulled by his voice as he took a step closer. His blue eyes were enticing and welcoming. This is probably how he got people to talk. One look, one smile and I was ready to confess–naked.

"And who is number one?" I asked as I watched his eyes trace over my face.

"You've heard about Dante's inferno right?" His low voice was pulling me closer. I nodded, afraid to speak. With Luca I had to tilt my head up to meet his eyes. That was something I wasn't used to. He must have been over 6'2. Mr. Costa was most likely six feet tall since it didn't take much to be eye level with him and I was only 5 '9.

"It is said that Dante's Inferno involves the nine circles of hell. Well my cousin has nine levels when it comes to…what he does. There's a reason that's his nickname," he said. He tugged at the tape measure around my neck and wicked thoughts began plaguing my mind. He hummed and his gaze darkened.

Then he gripped both ends and tugged hard. I gasped as I fell into his arms. My face flamed at the feel of his hard chest beneath my hands. The fabric of his suit jacket was soft. Did we make this one?

"You know my cousin isn't here yet. Maybe-" Luca's phone rang, breaking the tension. I leaned back quickly, heart pounding in my ears. Luca looked at me as he answered the phone. Nothing was going to happen. Nothing would have happened even if this blonde Italian god left my curiosity unfulfilled.

"Hello cousin," Luca said a bit loudly. I moved to gather some materials for the appointment. I needed to get space away from Luca and how he was making my body react.

A loud banging vibrated through the shop. I could make out Mr. Costa's voice loudly speaking about the door. He was leaning into the glass. His eyebrows were drawn in, his eyes blazed with annoyance.

"I don't know. I think she's safer locked in with me," Luca said, with a taunting smirk. I rolled my eyes. Mr. Costa began tugging at the door. The hinges creaked. I glared at Luca.

"If he breaks my door, he's not allowed in here," I snapped. Mr. Costa stepped away from the door. Sighing, I walked over to unlock it.

"You're no fun," Luca pouted slightly as Mr. Costa stomped in towards his cousin.

"I don't need a *'Whose Dick Is Bigger Than Whose'* especially with me in between," I said, crossing my arms. Luca smiled wickedly.

"Why are you alone with him?" Mr. Costa said, thrusting a finger in Luca's direction. His gray eyes looked tired. He had a frown on his face. I felt the need to wipe it away. I dug my fingers into my palms. I desperately needed to put batteries in my vibrator and lay off the mafia romances.

"You sent him to watch over me as if I'm a child," I stated. He looked over at Luca.

"I wouldn't leave him alone with you unless there was a 12 foot pole attached to him," Mr. Costa said. I glanced at Luca confused.

"I mean I have a-"

Mr. Costa's eyes cut Luca's sentence down. Luca straightened himself, looking away from his cousin. For some reason I felt like laughing. Luca in our conversation was easy going and yet Mr. Costa had the ability to shut him up.

"Well I'm leaving!" Luca said. "I was the perfect gentleman cousin. Don't worry." Luca clapped his hand on Mr. Costa's shoulder. He turned to face me and leaned towards my ear. His warmth breath sent shivers down my spine.

"For now," he said. My cheeks heated. And with those two words Luca was gone. The tense air seemed to dissipate.

Now I was alone with Mr. Costa and it was already seven. He looked at me up and down. He was probably noticing my rumpled oversized blouse, scuffed leggings and disheveled hair. He, on the other hand, was wearing a dress shirt, with fitted slacks. My eyes paused on the stain around his cufflink. My heart stopped. *Blood?*

I turned away, making a beeline for my materials. A thousand thoughts raced through my head. Had he hurt someone? Torture? Worse? Fuck and I was alone with him. A part of me was scared but also intrigued.

Mr. Costa followed me towards the dressing room. "What did my cousin tell you?" he asked. I bit my lip.

"Don't worry about it," I mumbled. His hand gently grabbed my shoulder turning me around and then moved to cupped my cheek. My eyes widened. What was he doing? His hand felt warm, gentle. His eyes bled with concern. How could someone who represented forms of darkness be so concerned with me? How could he be so gentle?

"Why are you touching me?" I asked. His eyes casted down before meeting my gaze.

"Tell me," he pleaded softly. I licked my lips.

"If your hand stays on my face I'm kicking you in the balls and then you won't be able to do anything with your dick," I said with a bite.

Instead of removing his hand, his fingers pushed into my hair. I bit the inside of my cheek, to keep my reaction at bay. His body was so close to mine. My focus began waning. I wanted his hand to tug my hair, to feel his muscles against my skin. His mouth was hovering slightly above mine, right there for me to take. Mr. Costa pulled away and the air around us cooled immediately.

"Usually that works," he said. I barked out a laugh.

"Did Mr. Bad Mafia Man really think that a gentle hand, a soft voice and batting those pretty gray eyes would make me tell you anything?" I asked. I placed his suit and pants in the dressing room. There was a tick in his jaw. Was I playing with fire? Absolutely. And I was enjoying it.

"Should I try a different approach, Cinderella? Do you prefer a firmer hand?" he asked with an eyebrow raised. "Want Mr. Bad Mafia Man as you put it, to force the truth out of you?" I tossed my hair over my shoulder, exposing my neck.

"Try it Mr. Costa," I said, offering myself to the wolf. His hand wrapped around my neck. He could feel my pulse drumming against his fingers. I did everything I could to keep a steady pulse. His pupils were beginning to dilate and his cheeks pinkened. His nostrils flared as he took in a breath.

"What did he tell you?" he asked, adding light pressure. I sucked in a breath. *Fuck.*

"Is that the best you can do?" I snickered.

"If I didn't know any better I'd say you like this," he said. His thumb stroked my vein. My whole body tensed, fighting itself. There was wetness gathering between my thighs and I was aching for relief.

"I wouldn't say that when you're threatening to cut off my air," I said. I sounded more breathless than I wanted to. His breath caressed my cheek and my eyes fluttered closed.

"If you can still form full sentences it's not a threat Cinderella," he whispered. Grabbing his wrist I stared into the wolf's eyes bravely.

"And clearly I'm not breaking so you can remove your hand now," I said. His response? A devilish smirk. His hand slid off of my throat, slowly, achingly as if imprinting his touch to my skin. "Thank you," I said. I stepped back and pointed to the dressing room.

"Strip and try these on," I said. He raised an eyebrow.

"No please?" he teased. I scoffed. His eyes never left mine and he kept the curtain open, providing me with a show. His tattoo caught my eye again.

I had seen the way it swirled up his leg and arched over the waistline of his boxers but what did the parts hidden beneath his underwear look like? I walked over, enticed by his tattoo once again.

"I didn't think that word would be in the dictionary of a man such as yourself," I said. He pulled his pants, slowly zipping them up. My eyes shamelessly watched.

"*Bella*, are you confusing me with the men in your books?" he asked.

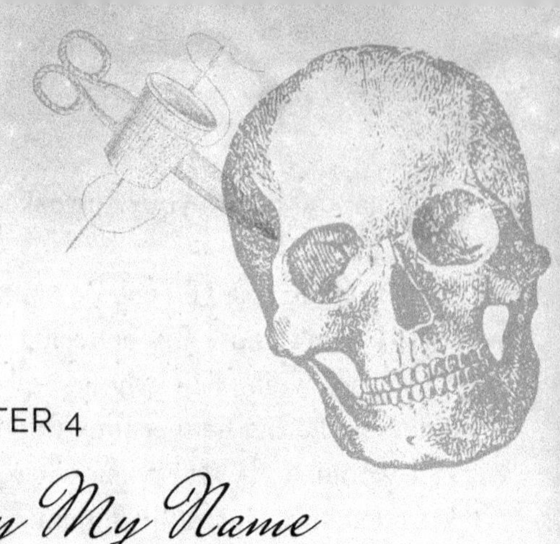

CHAPTER 4

Call Me By My Name

A NAME CAN BE A POWERFUL THING ESPECIALLY WHEN SAID IN A BREATHLESS MANNER

After pinning his jacket I left Mr. Costa to change back to his normal clothes. I would leave the jacket for tomorrow's to do list but was happy to have his pants at least done. The jacket just needed to be tightened in a few places. I stifled a yawn as I began putting everything away. Mr. Costa strolled out of the dressing area, typing away from his phone.

"I'll walk you to your car," he said. I nodded, too tired to form a sassy remark and in all honestly grateful. Ever since learning about the mafia I've felt on edge. I didn't want to walk outside in the dark alone constantly looking into the shadows.

It didn't take long to lock the shop up. We walked towards my car in silence. "I'll see you tomorrow," he said. I opened my car door.

"Excuse me?" I said. His eyebrows shot up.

"Excuse *me*?" he responded back. I pointed to my shop's door.

"Hours of operation are located on my door, in plain english and clearly states that we are closed on Sunday's," I said. He glanced over, his jaw tight.

"Well, what are you doing tomorrow?" he asked.

"I'm going to lounge around in sweats and bake bread," I said, throwing my bag into my passenger side. His tongue poked his cheek.

"I. Like. Bread," he struggled to get out. I raised an eyebrow.

"So?" I said. He rolled his eyes and pulled out his phone. He nodded absentmindedly and I turned away to get into my car. I hated being ignored and I wouldn't put up with his attitude. Mr. Costa's hands came on either side of me, gripping the top of my car. His chest pressed against my back and I bit back a moan.

"I'll see you tomorrow at 9 with coffee. *We* can bake bread," he said in a low voice. I turned my head to the side, catching his gaze. A black car with tinted windows rolled up from my peripheral.

"You don't know where I live," I said through clenched teeth. The nerve of this man. His chuckle vibrated against my chest.

"Cinderella, did you forget who I am?" he said.

"What if I don't want to be alone with you?" I asked. His fingers grazed my neck, pushing my hair back and exposing my neck.

"I highly doubt that," he said as his fingers stroked my neck. I squeeze my thighs to ease the throbbing this man created. Our chests brushed against each other and he had a dark gleam in his eyes.

"Really because your cousin said I should be careful around you," I said. He shook his head.

"Luca?" he said with a frown until his eyes ignited with a playful glint. "You should be careful around *us*. We can be trouble," he said.

"Double the trouble," I said. Mr. Costa hummed and he leaned to place a chaste kiss on my cheek. My fingers twitched to bring him closer.

And without another word he walked over to the black car. Turning around he waved at me to get into her car. I rolled my eyes, slamming my car door closed. I glanced one more time at Mr. Costa.

Tomorrow, he mouthed.

HE SHOWED up at nine sharp with two coffees. He was dressed in black sweats that had no right fitting his body the way they did. Was all of his clothes custom made?

I sighed deeply. I had stayed up fixing a few things on his jacket and hemming a dress. I glanced back at my apartment as he stood silently in front of me. I was hoping he was joking about showing up. But I was a fool to not believe the words of a mafia man.

"You look better this way," I said without thinking. He smiled. An actual smile that softened his face. Even though it was small it transformed him. A small tilt of his lips had the ability to bring me to my knees. I had never had someone look at me as if I hung the moon.

I looked away. If I continued memorizing the way his eyes melted and his full lips stretched it was going to make me give in. I was not going to fall for this mafia man even if my libido was screaming at me. Seriously, I needed to buy some damn batteries.

"You're nice in the morning," he said. I rolled my eyes and stepped away from the door allowing him in. Handing me one of the coffees he strolled in. His eyes wandered around, trying to grab every detail. It was like either he was assessing my place or searching for something. The short hallway opened into a small living room. The kitchen was just off to the side, a counter separating the space.

"Nice place," he said. I grunted, sipping my coffee. My nose twitched at the taste. I had never nor ever will be a morning person. Mr. Costa spoke two sentences and it was two sentences too long. I walked past the hallway mirror and cringed at my attire. I wore an old college sweatshirt with sweatpants covered in dried paint. My cheeks were flushed and my eyes were a little swollen.

My apartment felt much smaller with him in it. He seemed to suck the air out of every space he was in. I eyed him up and down. I wonder if that was a requirement of every mafia man.

Luca didn't really seem to give off that vibe. But he could be one of those people whose darkness hides behind his smile. I felt myself blush at the thought. These men were clouding my thoughts lately.

"How can I help?" His voice broke my train of thought. I shook my head.

"You sit there, I'll bake," I said. I had pointed to the bar stools in front of my kitchen counter.

"But I came to help," he insisted. I shook my head.

"It'll stress me out," I confessed. I couldn't stand having another person cook next to me. Having to watch myself cook and then keep an eye on the other person was stressful. He opened his mouth to say something and I raised a finger. I glared at him and he sat down quietly.

I was quickly becoming used to bossing this man around.

WE STAYED in silence as I began gathering the ingredients and tools to bake bread. Before my *avó* had passed she had begun passing me some recipes. I always enjoyed baking bread with her the most. I opened my fridge and frowned. If I had bacon and *linguiça* I could make *folar* but I would have to settle on regular artisan bread.

I heard shuffling from behind me. Mr. Costa had stood up. I looked up at him.

"Mr. Costa?" I said.

"I should leave you alone. You seem…comfortable," he said. My eyes widened at his statement. Now he was willing to leave me alone? I found myself chuckling at his behavior. I thought I had his type figured out but maybe there was more to him.

"And what else did you expect? Me to be shaking in my sweats because I have the big bad wolf in my kitchen?" I teased. The tips of his ears reddened and I smirked. So the big bad wolf could be flustered. Interesting. I walked over to him.

"I guess since you're here because you forcibly invited yourself into my home which said home's location was *not* given to you I'll put you to work," I said, placing my hands on my hips.

"Excuse me?" he said.

"You said you wanted to help. Now while I am perfectly fine at baking bread on my own there is something else you can do for me Mr. Costa," I said. He eyed me warily which was a good thing.

My mom and *avó* taught me a few lessons before passing. A Portuguese woman can get anyone to do anything with the promise of food. So if this man wanted bread he was going to work for it. A rush of exhilaration coursed through my body.

"I HOPE you realized Ms. Silva that I am not a maid," he hissed. While his voice may have sounded scary to anyone it had the opposite effect on me. I stood off to the side, watching him.

"If the whole mafia thing doesn't work out you would make an excellent house cleaner. You were very thorough with my ceiling fans and I appreciate it," I said with a pleasant smile. He leaned in until our noses brushed.

I stood staring at him in amazement. I should be scared right now. I should be terrified that a man of his nature was in my apartment.

Hell, I never gave him the address. For some reason none of that phased me. His nose twitched slightly. I smirked. I enjoyed putting a man like Mr. Costa in his place.

"I cleaned your ceiling fans, air vents and tops of your cabinets. What am I going to get in return?" he asked.

"I'm baking bread which you can take with you," I said, nonchalantly. He let out a dark chuckle.

"Bread for cleaning? Really?" he said in disbelief. I glared at him.

"I already have one day left to make your suit. I've been working overtime for you. I think this is the least you can do Mr. Costa," I said.

"I'm paying you for your service," he pointed out.

"Yes you are because we have a professional relationship despite the fact you found my address and showed up at my apartment. Is there something else you want from me"? I asked. His eyes traveled down to my lips.

"You intrigue me…Lucia," he said, softly. My heart rattled in my chest. My hands grew clammy and my stomach twisted. My name on his lips was like a calling card, luring me to walk on the darker side. The way he said my name was…erotic. I wanted him to say it again.

"That last thing I want is to be intriguing to someone of the Costa family," I said. His hands clenched against the kitchen sink. Staring into his eyes, my stomach twisted.

"I cannot change where I come from the same way you cannot," he said. I nodded.

"We come from different places," I said, sounding almost breathless. Mr. Costa tilted his head.

"If that is what you think," he said softly. My throat closed. I didn't like what he was insinuating. There was a secret beneath his words. Staring into his eyes I was reminded of the questions that I had. Mr. Costa held the answers. I just needed to find a way to get them.

"What do you want in return?" I asked, caving. Clearly he was a man who didn't do anything just for the hell of it but for something in return.

"Call me Dante."

I sat up on the kitchen counter, my eyes focused on *Dante*. I had been purposely calling Dante Mr. Costa to keep some form of professionalism with him. I wanted to keep a wall with him.

I watched him roll up his sleeves, exposing his tan forearms. I could faintly make out a tattoo on his right arm. An emblem of some sorts. He dipped his hands in the hot water and continued scrubbing. His hands were hard at work and I found myself fantasizing about what they could do to me.

"I didn't know what coffee you liked so I asked the barista and she suggested pumpkin spice." Dante spoke in a soft voice. "It's in season," he said. I smiled.

"I actually don't like pumpkin spice," I said. Dante nearly dropped the sponge.

"You've been drinking it this whole time," he pointed out, looking at me in shock.

"I actually only took one sip," I said. He sighed.

"My coffee is black. I haven't touched it yet. Heat it up and add some milk," he offered. I shook my head.

"And you?" I asked. He threw me a killer smile that stopped my heart and made me squeeze my thighs. Fuck his pretty face. This man was making the wall I constructed crumble.

"I secretly like pumpkin spice," he said. I threw back my head in a full laugh. A man who could kill secretly liked pumpkin spice coffee of all things. Every time I thought I had him peg he said something that threw me off. Dante's eyes softened as he watched me. My cheeks grew warm as he stared at me. There was more to this bad wolf than I thought.

I stirred my new cup of coffee and smiled while Dante was busy drying dishes. His character was interesting. I could tell from our first interaction he was a man who was made of steel. He liked things done his way and he didn't put up with anyone's crap. He did his best to not put up with my attitude.

However, even though the man before me was dark and dangerous, there was a sweet side to him. He helped clean my fucking apartment and liked pumpkin spice coffee. While I gave him shit and bossed him around he begrudgingly did what I asked.

I took a deep breath. So much had fucking happened in such a short time. Why wasn't I freaking out more? Dante glanced at me and winked. I flushed.

I've always held a fire within me and typically it was something that I tried to keep tame. I was always getting in trouble for being blunt and impulsive. But the fire Dante had rivaled my own. He ignited me in more ways than one. With him I wasn't afraid to burn.

"Let's watch a movie," I suggested. The bread was still baking and we had time to waste until then. Dante glanced at the couch in the living room. He nodded slowly, grabbing his coffee. We both sat on opposite sides, placing space between us. This was professional right?

I grimaced. Nothing about this was professional. It's not like I was going to work on his suit. It was my day off. Therefore there was no reason for him to be here. He was a client sitting on my couch.

I threw on a random movie knowing full well I wouldn't be able to concentrate with him there. I had too many questions in my head. It's why my sleep schedule was even more fucked up than normal. I looked over at Dante.

He casually took up the corner of the couch, his long legs splayed out. One arm hung back. His angle was basically an invitation to cuddle. Did mafia men cuddle?

I cursed at my thoughts. He was a part of the mafia. Part of the world my *avô* was tangled in and kept hidden from me. I felt conflicted with what he was versus with what he continued to show me. I glanced over at him for the hundredth time.

"Something you wanna say?" His storm colored eyes were playful.

You mean do.

"Do?" he questioned. I stiffened. I hadn't realized I said it out loud. This time he adjusted himself closer to me.

"What do you wanna do?" His tone was low and playful. My heart fluttered. How many sides of him was he going to show me today? First it was his usual grumpy self, then a softer side and now a playful one. What did I want to do? I wanted to kiss him, ask him questions, and finish his suit. I blushed. Dante shifted closer.

"Come on Lucia. Tell me. What is it you want to do?" he asked again. He needed to stop saying my name goddammit. But it had been so long since I've been with someone.

I had an itch that needed to be scratched and it was all his stupid fault with his muscles, gray eyes and tattoos. I wanted to feel his lips glide against mine, feel his hands rough against my skin.

But that would mean giving into him, into temptation. Dante was enticing that's for sure. I was afraid that kissing him would be the first step into his inferno and once there, there was no going back.

"From the look in your eyes I think you know," I said. He offered a crooked smile that twisted my panties.

"I want to hear you say it," he demanded. He was leaning closer this time. The movie at this point was nothing but background noise. His other hand landed on my knee, tracing circles. Even through the fabric my body was beginning to burn.

"If I say it out loud it might happen," I said. My tone is on the verge of needy and I hated that. I hated how he made me want him. He was so close I could smell his smokey pine cologne. It was making my head spin.

"Do you want it to happen?" he asked softly. His hand slowly went up my thigh. I fought the urge to roll my eyes back. It really has been so fucking long since I've been touched by someone that wasn't me.

My eyes could only focus on his lips. Should I? Maybe I should give myself a break and enjoy some fun. Just forget the world and just revel in the sensation for a bit.

I stared into Dante's eyes. They were tempting me. He wanted me to give in. His hand scorched a trail higher up on my thighs. My body trembled beneath his hand. I leaned in, following the thread that was pulling us in. But then a phone rang interrupting us. He let out a curse in Italian.

"Let me take this," he said, standing up and heading to the kitchen. After a few hushed words he came back out. "I have to head out to handle…something," he said. I nodded. The need to touch him disappeared like a candle being blown out. I watched Dante walk out my door to do unspeakable things.

And now I needed to reconcile with myself over the fact that I almost gave into Dante Costa.

CHAPTER 5

Long Distance Phone Calls

DON'T START A GAME IF YOU'RE NOT READY TO PLAY...

Dante had walked out the door and I laid back on the couch, staring at the ceiling. I covered my face with my hand. I felt conflicted. I wasn't supposed to be feeling this way with Dante and yet I was. Dante was every mother's nightmare. Actually he was worse. He was the thing that gave nightmares.

My phone rang and I jumped. My heart dropped for a second. Flipping over my phone my stomach twisted in knots. It was my *avô*. I had questions and this man could answer them.

"Bom dia!" I said brightly.

"Lucia," he warned. Fuck.

"Avô," I responded in the same tone. He sighed.

"You know I know," he said. I grimaced. I wasn't going to question what he meant. Growing up it was difficult to keep secrets when everyone knew everyone. And yet he managed to keep a big one.

He made it sound as if I was in trouble when he was the one in the hot seat. I took a deep breath because two could play at this game.

"I also know about you know what," I said, leaning back against the couch. He was not going to make me feel guilty about something I was purposely kept away from. He grumbled, clearly in the wrong.

"It's not something I wanted to keep from you," he said. Tears pricked my eyes. But he did. He kept a lot from me. Everything I knew about my family was basically a lie and yet I still felt like I was missing pieces of a puzzle. "*Eu sinto muito*. I should have told you. There's still so much for you to know," he said.

"Then tell me what I need to know right now," I pleaded. He hesitated.

"We work for the mafias," he said. I dug my hand into the couch and gritted my teeth. The last thing I wanted was for my voice to reveal any kind of weakness.

"You mean all of them? They come to the shop?" I asked.

"For the past 15 years or so," he said. My brain raced. This has been going on for years, right under my nose.

"Why?" I asked. He cleared his throat. I didn't give a shit if this made him uncomfortable. I needed to know the truth.

"There was an agreement years ago," he said, firmly.

"What kind of agreement? Why?" I pushed. He sighed heavily.

"*Minha vida* I have to go. But I promise to tell you everything when I can," he said. Convenient that he had to leave. I swallowed. At least he admitted to working for the mafia.

"Is there anything important I should know until then?" I asked quickly. I needed him to give something, any morsel of truth so I didn't feel like I was walking on eggshells. Nerves erupted all over my skin.

"Just be careful and Dante…," he trailed off. My cheeks flamed at the mention of his name. From Dante's point of view he had a nice relationship with my *avô*.

"*Sim*?" I said, feeling my body tighten up. I could hardly breathe as I waited for him to speak.

"Trust him," he said before hanging up.

THE BREAD WAS COOLING on the kitchen counter and the movie ended a while ago. I rested my head against the couch cushion. Trust him? My lying *avô* was telling me to trust a man whose career involved lurking in the shadows.

How could I? A part of me wanted to run away from Dante and yet there was something pulling me towards him. With every stitch of his suit I was becoming more attracted to him. His long fit body, the tattoos that he kept hidden. He was weaving his way into my heart.

I must be crazy.

He's a dangerous man who does dangerous things and my family worked for him. I chewed my bottom lip. Maybe I just needed to scratch an itch. Clearly he didn't mind. And maybe I could get answers from Dante. An idea arose as a strong knock vibrated through my apartment.

I froze for a second before making my way towards the door. I reached for the baseball bat that laid in the corner. My hands tightened around the wood. I frowned at the weight. A metal bat might be more useful considering everything happening.

Looking into the peephole the devil stood on the opposite side. I relinquished the bat. Taking a deep breath I opened the door to find him leaning against the opposite wall, dinner in hand. The smell smacked me in the face and made my mouth water. The food wasn't the only thing making me drool though.

Dante stood in a black t-shirt and gray sweatpants. I bit the inside of my cheek at the way his gray sweatpants wrapped around his muscular thighs. I forced my eyes to his face and not the bulge his sweatpants teased. His left cheek was slightly bruised and my stomach dropped. The bruise was a reminder of what he was. He left to do gods know what to someone.

My fingers, on their own accord, brushed the sensitive skin. Dante didn't flinch and for some reason that hurt more.

"Are you okay?" I asked. His lips twitched and he leaned against my doorway.

"Careful Cinderella, you almost sound like you care," he murmured. I pulled my hand away and rolled my eyes.

"Despite what you think I do have a heart," I said.

"And despite what *you* think I do as well," he said. My heart fluttered. He did, didn't he? He walked me to my car, brought me food and cleaned my apartment. Despite it all there was a heart beneath his hard exterior.

"I still have to try the bread right?" he said, breaking my thoughts. He held up the bag.

"I suppose," I said with a shrug. I turned my back and left the door open for him to follow. A tiny part of me was happy he had come back. I was craving his presence but now I could begin my plan.

I walked towards the kitchen, knowing he would follow me. I sat on top of my counter and he placed the food next to me before forcing his way between my legs. I raised an eyebrow.

"Is it Italian?" I asked, gesturing towards the bag. His eyes traveled up my body slowly. My body reacted under his watchful eye. His hands skimmed up my thighs and goosebumps erupted all over my body. He was making me lose focus again.

"I wanted to eat Portuguese tonight," he said. I stared at him in shock and then burst out laughing. His eyes widened. "That's not the reaction I was expecting," he grumbled. I smiled at him.

"That's the line the big mafia man decides to go with?" I teased. He glared at me.

"You're lucky I find you interesting," he said. I gingerly ran my fingers up his arm, my eyes following the trail before meeting his gaze. He watched me, slightly guarded.

"And why is that," I said, my voice sounding slightly breathy. He stepped in closer, his hips aligning with mine. I fought back a moan at the feel of his hard body.

"I should bend you over and punish you for all the disrespect and back talk," he said as his lips brushed the shell of my ear. My heart banged against my chest.

"Sounds more like a reward than a punishment," I said as my arms snaked around his neck. I just needed him to lower his guard slightly so I could get information out of him. His lips grazed my throat and my eyes fluttered closed. I let out a soft gasp when I felt his teeth. His hands dug into my hips.

Dante is flushed against my body. Every instinct inside of me is roaring to rock for relief. My core is throbbing, begging for attention.

"You're playing a dangerous game," he warned, pulling away. I stared into his gray eyes and a startling resolution struck me. I *was* playing a game. But I intended to win. I was going to figure out all the details between my family and the mafias and I was going to tear it apart. And Dante was going to help me.

His hand slipped into my hair and lightly tugged. My body shivered against my will. My eyes fluttered close and his lips traced the shell of my ear again.

"Looks like you like that," he said, voice deep and tempting. His teeth nibbled my earlobe and it took every ounce of control to not wrap my legs around his waist and bring him closer.

"You have no idea what I like and while I'd enjoy having you discover what they are, I'm really hungry," I said, hopping off the counter and standing behind him. I pushed him to unpack the food and he grunted. He handed me a container.

"Gumbo," he stated. The perfect pairing for my bread. He glanced over his shoulder.

"That's perfect," I said, food replacing my thoughts on mafia men.

SITTING across from him I glanced at his bruised cheek. Horrible scenarios began racing through my head. Imagine, being with someone in his line of work. This is how it would be. Sharing meals with someone who was constantly covered in blood and bruises. Could I even stomach that? He placed his spoon down.

"Ask," he said with annoyance. I sighed.

"Why do you do it?" I asked.

He responded nonchalantly, "someone has too."

I glared at him and stood up. People have to die? For what? Money? Drugs? Anger coursed through my veins. Did it mean he didn't care about who he hurt, killed or worse? Did he not care about the lives his *job* affected?

"We can't keep doing this," I spat out. Within a few days I had deluded myself in falling for this man. I got swept up by his shadows. I was enticed by the fire behind his gray eyes.

I didn't look at him. I knew if I did I would cave. We shouldn't be spending time together. He was a client. He was the mafia. And yet my *avô* trusted him and wanted *me* to trust him.

Dante got up, following me into the kitchen. "Doing what?" he asked. I began doing the dishes, needing a task to keep myself busy.

"Don't pretend to not know what I'm talking about. This thing between us can't happen. I won't put myself or the people I care about in danger because of you or your family," I said.

Even though my *avô* told me to trust him, books and life taught me one thing and that is people could easily go back on their word. I needed to break the agreement my family had with the mafias.

I was surprised by the anger that was coursing through my veins. My control was snapping. Between my growing feelings for Dante's, Luca's enchanting blue eyes and the mafias everything felt like it was catching up to me.

I felt his chest against my back. His hands slipped over mine to grab the sponge. His fingers tangled with mine as we washed the dishes in tangent.

"And what's between us?" he asked, his lips tickling my ear. He rested his chin on my shoulder. I rinsed the dishes and placed them on the rack. Dante slid his wet hands up my arm, inciting goosebumps.

"What. Are. We?" he asked, turning me around. His eyes were serious and that wall around my heart was rumbling.

"You know what I'm referring to," I said. He pressed his hips into mine and I bit the inside of my cheek. It was terrifying how easily he made my body come alive.

"Not the answer I'm looking for," he said in a low voice. I bit back a moan. He tilted my chin. I could use this to my advantage. Dante Costa was interested in me and instead of running away from it I was going to use it. He tapped my forehead.

"Are you still there?" he asked.

"I'm not starting anything," I said, looking away. Dante represented freedom, impulse, desire and most importantly answers. His hand slid back into my hair and he yanked harder this time. My eyes fluttered closed.

"You start and I'll make sure you finish," he whispered against my throat. With his face buried in my neck I stared at the ceiling with a smirk. Let the games begin.

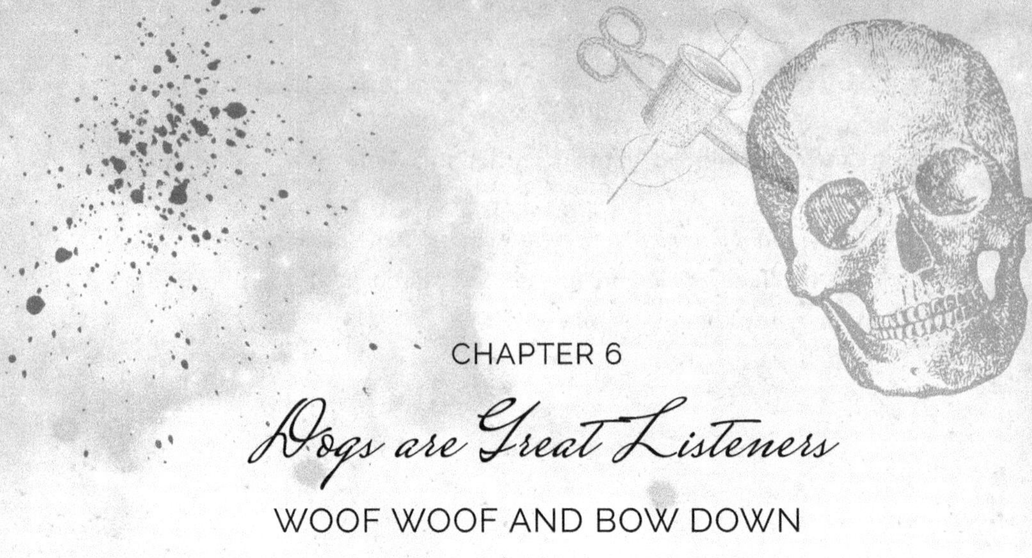

CHAPTER 6

Dogs are Great Listeners

WOOF WOOF AND BOW DOWN

I stared into his lust-filled eyes. His eyes traveled up and down my body, slowly. He was waiting. He needed me to make the first move since I was the one who was unsure. But I wasn't going to hesitate anymore.

I watched the way his eyes drunk me in. It was like he was memorizing every part of me. A sense of power coursed through my body. I was going to have this man so tightly wound around my pinky he wouldn't be able to make a move without thinking of how it would affect me.

"Fuck it," I whispered. I faintly heard him gasp as I took his face in my hands. I smashed my lips against his, causing him to stumble back. He quickly recovered his balance and matched my fury. I relaxed in his arms, giving myself up to the tidal wave of lust. He pushed me back against the sink counter.

My fingers twisted into his hair, tugging. His sweatpants provided little barrier to what I could feel. His hands dug into my waist. I bit his lower lip and slightly pulled away. He groaned beautifully.

"Fuck," he whispered against my mouth. Our tongues clumsily found their way into a tango that set me on fire. But I wanted more. It had been so long since I felt like this and I had never been with a man who was this detailed with his tongue.

His hands stayed gripping my hips and I wanted him to touch me. I knew he was being cautious but I was taking a jump. I wasn't the type to tentatively give in. When I decided to do something I went all the way.

So I did the next lustful logical thing. I widened my legs, allowing him more room. I pushed my lips against his, forcing him to get on my level.

Instinctively he pushed back as he nipped and licked up and down my neck. I shut my eyes closed, letting the sensations wash over me. His hands were greedy as they kneaded my thighs. I desperately wanted between my legs. My core ached to be touched.

"More," I whispered, dragging one of his hands up my body. He forcibly stopped his hand from getting closer to her breast. "More," I pleaded. He looked into my eyes, pupils dilated, breathing ragged. His swollen lips pouted.

"Can we go to the couch?" he asked. Mhmm, manners were sexy. I nodded. He smirked, slipping his hands under my ass to lift me. I wrapped my legs tight around his waist and moaned at the feeling of his erection.

Instead of laying me down he sat, keeping me on top. I gasped at feeling him fully beneath my hips. I rocked against him. Dante threw his head back, eyes closed in bliss. I dragged my hands up his chest, gripping his neck.

"Look at me," I demanded. His eyes collided with mine. His mouth hung open as I pushed my nails into his hair. I leaned down and pressed kisses against his neck. I sucked on his neck hard before soothing it with my tongue. He moaned again, his hands massaging my ass. I had control and it was giving me a delicious high.

"Lucia," he hissed. I smirked. I liked watching him become undone. I could see his control slowly slipping and dammit if it wasn't the hottest thing ever. He finally opened his eyes. Our gazes locked. His fingers slipped underneath the hem of my shirt, lightly grazing my skin. I arched on instinct, needing to feel more of his hands on my bare skin.

He raised an eyebrow in question, again, wanting permission. I nodded eagerly. He began lifting up my shirt and then a phone blared. I jumped back, heart hammering. The phone popped our sexually charged bubble. I was two seconds from tossing that phone into the garbage can.

"Pick it up," I murmured and moved off his lap. Dante stood up, adjusting himself. I shamelessly watched and bit my lip. He felt really fucking good underneath me.

He cursed in Italian. He stared at his phone, taking a deep breath. The ringing phone had spiked my adrenaline and depleted it just as fast.

I made my way to the kitchen to repackage the food. I could faintly hear him from across the room. The words were jumbled, a mix of English and Italian. His shoulders were hitched up and his fist was clenched.

I wondered what was wrong. I looked away, needing a moment to catch my breath. My body was still tingling. I was so close to giving myself over to Dante and I would have. I jumped feeling his arm around my waist. He kissed my cheek.

"We'll finish this later," he murmured. Turning in his grasp I squinted at him.

"This was your one chance," I said. A muscle in his jaw ticked. I smiled inwardly. I was going to leave him wanting more, needing me. The string was slowly being wrapped around him.

"Like I said once you finish and you haven't," he said. He did say that. He placed a kiss on my neck and lightly bit the pulsing vein, sending instant shivers down my spine. "I promise," he whispered against my skin. He walked out the door once again.

The chess pieces were moving.

THE NEXT DAY was Dante's final fitting. Once I handed over the suit there was nothing keeping us from speaking to each other. I couldn't let that happen. There were things I needed to know. We stood in the back of the shop. Dante began stripping down and my pulse quickened.

"I'll give you some privacy," I said, turning away. He pulled me flush against him and dragged me into the empty changing room. His lips teased my ear.

"You've seen me half naked before," he mumbled. "And didn't I say once you finish?" he said. I stared into his gray eyes. They were playful, filled with hunger. The invisible string hung loosely around his shoulders. His fingers traced a line from my temples, down the side of my cheek, under my jaw and down my neck.

"Stop thinking," he said, voice gravelly. I bit my bottom lip. He pulled my bottom lip from my teeth. "I want to be the one to do that," he murmured. His warmth wrapped around me like an embrace.

"Dante..." I said softly. He closed his eyes as if savoring the sound of his name on my lips. He pressed me against the wall. My hips bucked on their own accord. One hand tightened on my hip. The other, gripping the back of my neck. My heart was racing. My hands were itching to weave their way through his silky dark hair.

"Don't make me beg, Lucia," he said, waiting. There was a needy edge to his voice. Something in me snapped. I placed my hands on his chest and pushed him against the opposite wall, pressing myself against him. His eyes half closed in a low moan. I gripped his jaw in my hand. His eyes snapped open, hungry. I needed to know how far I could push his control. I needed to know how much of him I owned.

"Maybe that's what I want. Maybe I want to show you what it's like to be at the mercy of someone else and wipe that entitled smirk off your face," I said as my hand dragged roughly down his button shirt. My hand trailed further south, brushing the tent in his pants. Dante took a deep breath, his eyes focused on my lips.

"This is what's going to happen. You're going to try on this damn suit so I can be done with it and maybe I'll consider inviting you over tonight to finish what I started," I said.

AFTER TRYING on the suit I made a mental note of the things I needed to fix. Luckily it wasn't much. I felt a pain on the side of my head forming again.

So naturally like any workaholic I ignored it and settled in the chair by the cash register to make my to do list. Dante strolled out from the back of the store. His eyes assessed me as if he knew something was off.

"Just a headache. I'm fine," I said, waving him off. The look in his eyes showed he wanted to say something but instead he held back. His phone rang. Glancing at the screen he pocketed his phone and kissed my cheek in goodbye.

I sighed, being able to breathe. I needed to try to get answers from him tonight. I stared at my phone debating whether or not to call my *avô*. I shook my head. I wasn't going to interrupt him.

The suit needed to be done for tomorrow and so I shifted my focus on that. I carried on with my day, sewing, cutting, stabbing myself with a pin every once in a while. The pain in my head however was getting worse and I knew it was too late to take any medicine.

I mentally cursed at myself. This was leading towards a migraine and I should have paid more attention. The consistent headaches and stress were a sign of its impending doom.

I locked up the shop because there was no way I would be able to work through this. I learned that the hard way when I nearly stitched my index finger with the sewing machine. I just needed to get home and lay in bed.

I walked to my car with shaky legs. The brightness from the setting sun felt like nails railing into my head. The sound of cars driving by felt like an elephant stomping inside my skull. I breathed through my nose slowly.

I unlocked my car and someone called out to me. I turned around and the figure walking towards me was standing in front of the sun, blinding me and sending a wave of nausea. Fuck. They had to pick that spot. I leaned against her car.

"Are you okay?" a familiar voice asked.

"Yeah, yeah," I replied weakly. Another shot of pain barreled against my skull. I bit my lip to keep myself from crying out in pain. I unknow-ingly reached for his arm.

"Are you sure Lucia?" the voice asked. I continued to reach for him and felt his arm beneath my hand. I caught a whiff of citrus and cedar. I felt myself relax beneath this person. "Don't worry, I'll take care of you."

I WOKE up in my own bed. I gingerly sat up and grabbed my head immediately. Fuck, it didn't matter how careful I was sitting up, there was still a lingering pain. How did I get here? My bedroom door was slightly ajar and I could hear someone in my kitchen. Who the fuck was in my apartment?

All I could remember was a familiar voice calling to me and being carried inside. I placed my feet on the floor carefully, not wanting to upset my stomach. I didn't need the nauseous acting up.

Taking a deep breath I stood up. The door opened wider and it was Luca. My shoulders sagged in relief. I guess I didn't need to punch anyone for breaking into my apartment. Although given the state I was in earlier I think I had known it was Luca that saved me.

He was wearing a gray polo tucked into dark slimming slacks. His blonde hair was loose around his face in waves.

"How did you know where I—mafia," I said, closing my eyes. He offered a small smile. In his hands were a wet towel and a cup of tea.

"Why don't you lay back down?" His voice was gentle. I squinted at him. I wasn't sure why he was being nice. Did Dante send him? Unlike Dante, Luca had been kind from the beginning. There was an easy air around him that relaxed me. "You're not the first person I've left speech-less," he said with an easy smile. I sighed. I moved to sit on the edge of the bed as he walked over.

"You can leave now," I said, my voice scratching against my ears. He softly scoffed, setting the tea on my bedside. The smell of ginger and lemon hung in the air. Ginger was good for nauseous which happened whenever I had a migraine.

"I'm not leaving," he said, taking a seat next to me. The bed shifted under his weight. I should be nervous even scared that a slightly strange man was in my apartment and sitting on my bed but I wasn't. My lips twitched.

"You look like you're about to laugh," he pointed out. My cheeks heated.

"I just thought about how you're on my bed and Dante hasn't even made it towards my bedroom door," I said. Luca's eyes sparkled.

"Mhmm you sure know how to make a man feel good," he said with a lopsided grin. I couldn't stop myself from returning the same smile.

"You should leave," I whispered. I tilted my head at him. His eyes looked lighter like the sky on a clear day. They were warm and inviting. He placed the towel on my forehead. I hissed at the contact. The coolness instantly relaxed me.

"I can't leave you when you're like this," he said softly, leaning closer. I noticed many dots on the outskirts of his face. I felt the urge to trace them with my finger.

"I've dealt with this before," I said as he provided delicious pressure with the towel.

"Just because you're used to doing this alone doesn't mean you have to," he whispered. He rubbed slow lazy circles on my temples. "You also realized if I wasn't there you would have been passed out on the street," he pointed out. I rolled my eyes through the pain.

"I would have made it into my car if you hadn't called my name," I said. He chuckled while shaking his head.

"You can leave," I said, reaching for the towel. He continued staring at me. He was as stubborn as Dante. I sighed. "Fine you can stay out in the living room," I said, pointing towards the door. He glanced at my bed.

"I don't know your bed looks pretty comfy," he said, patting the mattress.

"It's for one person," I said. He let out a chuckle. It wasn't as deep as Dante's but I couldn't help but be slightly entranced by the sound.

"I could sit on the floor," he said, glancing at the spot by my window. I couldn't stop the smile from spreading across my face.

"Like a dog?" I teased. His eyes widened and a spark of excitement briefly coursed through me.

"Are you my master?" he asked. My cheeks flushed. My plan had briefly involved seducing Dante to get him to talk but Luca might be an easier route.

"Would you mind having a woman tell you what to do?" I asked. I placed the towel on my nightstand. He stared at me in silence as I crawled under my covers, settling in my bed. Luca didn't answer and so I decided to ask another question.

"Does Dante know?" I asked. I reached for my tea and took a sip. I hissed at the burning liquid. Luca leaned forward, hands on either side of me.

"I haven't decided if I want to tell him yet," he said and then blew a breath to cool down my tea. My eyes were trained on his lips. They were a dusty rose and his top lip was slightly fuller. I swallowed and nodded in thanks. I took another sip and enjoyed the taste. Luca smirked and made his way to the window. He sat down, crossed legged.

"Lucia," he called out from his position. I glanced at him as I buried myself beneath the covers.

"Yes, Luca?" I asked.

"Woof."

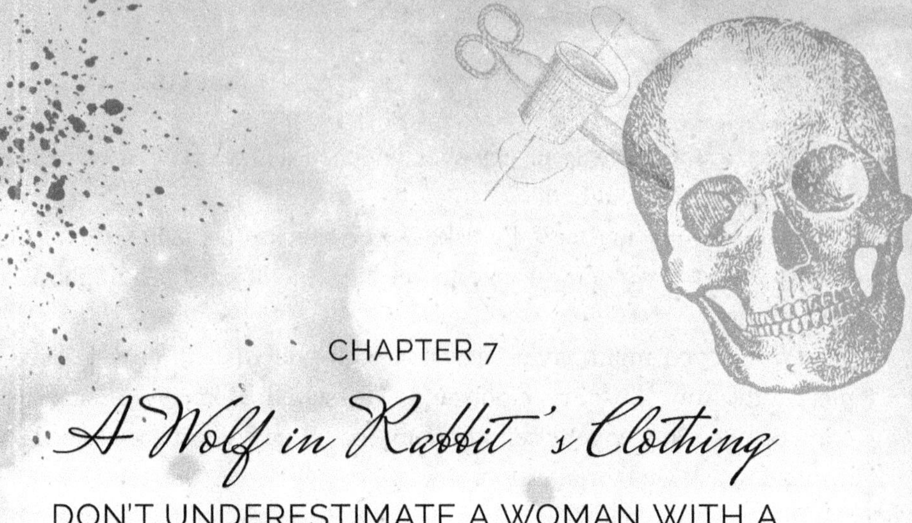

CHAPTER 7

A Wolf in Rabbit's Clothing

DON'T UNDERESTIMATE A WOMAN WITH A PRETTY SMILE

I fell asleep again and woke up to darkness. The only light was coming from the crack of my bedroom door. I could faintly hear Luca in the kitchen. I stood up and switched out of my clothes. I tugged on an old shirt and leggings.

Staring at the bed I made a mental note I would have to wash the sheets before bed. With the pain of my migraine subsiding my head now felt numb and drowsy.

Stepping into my living room I was surprised to see Dante, in my kitchen. Cooking. He turned around, surprised.

"Should you be up?" he asked quietly.

"Probably not but the pain is gone. I just feel drowsy," I said, my eyes still squinting at the light. He sighed in relief and went back to the pot on the stove. "Where's Luca?" I asked, making my way towards the kitchen.

"He called and told me what happened. I don't know much about migraines. Broken bones and bullets yes. Migraines? Nothing. But my *Nona's* chicken soup always makes everyone feel better." He kept his voice soft and low. I tried not to focus on the words *broken, bones,* or *bullets.* I felt taken aback though.

"That's really sweet of you," I said hesitating. He moved away from the pot to place a kiss on the side of my head.

"It's my fault for giving you a time crunch. And with everything that has been happening, all the stress." He sighed in disappointment. "Go sit on the couch and I'll bring you food and water," he said quietly.

"I mean I think I've been handling everything pretty well," I murmured. He cupped my cheek and I leaned into his comfort. I placed a hand on his chest, feeling his steady heartbeat. His eyes crinkled on the sides.

Through the fog clouding my brain I could see the softness of Dante for what it was. Authentic, raw and real. My rattled against my chest as a feeling long forgotten began slowly spreading. Dante pressed a gentle kiss on my forehead.

"Head to the couch and let me take care of you," he whispered. I sighed, sagging into his body.

"I'll listen to you this one time," I replied, my head buried in his chest. I didn't want to argue. Maybe I was too tired to but a part of me enjoyed this. I spent so long taking care of myself and others I didn't know what this felt like. As much as I intrigued Dante, his gentle side intrigued me.

Dante brought over a bowl and settled next to me on the couch. The bowl was warm in my hands. The smell was enchanting. I took a bite and moaned. Dante sighed. The soup tasted amazing and it was exactly what I needed.

After a few more bites I looked at him. "I have a serious question," I said, narrowing my eyes. Dante crossed his arms as he leaned against the couch cushion. He nodded for me to speak. "If I give you a family recipe can you give me this recipe?" I asked. He choked on a laugh, shaking his head.

"You don't have to give me something in return. I'll give it to you freely," he said. My eyebrows furrowed.

"You're not the type of person to just hand things out," I said.

"What can I say? You casted a spell on me," he said. I snorted.

"How?" I asked. A part of me was fishing for compliments and I didn't care. I wanted to know how I, a simple seamstress, grabbed the attention of a man of his nature. He raised an eyebrow.

"Are you doubtful of your charm? I didn't think of you as someone who needed their ego stroked," he said. I blushed in embarrassment.

"I'm confident in who I am and what I'm capable of," I said, staring into the bowl.

"But?"

"I'm not used to this," I said, pointing between us. "Ignoring the part that you're in the mafia—this isn't something I do," I confessed. Dante shifted on the couch and tapped my cheek. I met his steady gaze.

"You are beautiful. Fierce, loyal and brave. It's not hard to fall for you when you make it easy," he said. I sucked in a breath, staring wide eyed. I had never had someone say such words in a sweet way filled with conviction. A tiny part of me hated that his words touched me so much, that I craved them. I took a spoonful of the soup eyeing him carefully.

"Would you give me anything freely?" I said, going back to the original conversation. His eyes flickered between me and the TV. He scratched the scruff on his cheek before answering.

"I like this side of you," he said.

"What side?" I asked curiously. Dante leaned over and his fingers swept a piece of my hair back behind my ear.

"The side that thinks she can take control," he said. Defiance sluggishly swept through me. The drowsiness was still coursing through me. I set the soup on the table.

This wasn't how I wanted to play our game. Yes I liked control. It wasn't something I had often. Dante knew I had it which is why he kept giving in. Therefore I needed to figure out all of this mafia shit soon.

"Do I need to remind you of how I put you in your place?" I said. He leaned closely and despite my brain running at 5mph my body responded immediately.

"Do I have to remind you that I let you put me in my place?" he said. His cheeks were slightly flushed and his pupils were dilating. I smirked.

"So you enjoy it? Me putting you in your place, me having control," I said. Dante's nostrils flared. Got him.

"Cinderella, you need to watch what you're saying," he warned.

"Why?" I asked innocently. I was secretly a wolf pretending to be a rabbit. Dante's eyebrows furrowed.

"You had a massive migraine, you need to let your body relax," he said, pulling back.

I grabbed the soup from the table and settled back into the couch. He was right and it annoyed me. He let out a sigh and leaned over to carefully dust kisses all over my face. I felt every inch of me relax into the cushions. From my forehead, over each eye, my nose, across my cheeks until he hung right above my lips. I tilted back, waiting. I wanted him to kiss me. But would he still want me even after I severed my family's agreement with his?

I felt the brush of his lips as he whispered, "maybe I do like it."

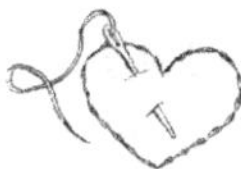

THE NIGHT ENDED with a kiss on the cheek and I slept on the couch. The next day the suit was ready for the big charity event. I was a bit annoyed that the event was taking place during the week. Did no one work the next day? I chuckled to myself. Of course the people at this event could afford having the next day off considering their bank accounts.

I typed away a few orders I needed when my *avô* called to check in. My heart was pounding. My grandpa's calls were now giving me major anxiety.

"Lucia," his warm voice echoed in the phone.

"*Olá avô*. How is it going?" I asked. I needed to act normal before asking the questions that have plagued my brain.

"It's good. I picked up some extra clients," he said. I nodded along. "How is the shop?" he asked. I snorted.

"You mean the shop that seems to provide outfits for the mafias?" I asked. Yeah sugarcoating was never my strong suit. He sighed.

"We couldn't have a few more minutes of normal conversation?" he teased. I couldn't help but giggle.

"And risk you mysteriously hanging up? Nope," I said, moving my way to the back of the store. He sighed again.

"There are some things I can't say over the phone," he said. I furrowed my brows. Was it because someone could be listening in?

"You said I could trust Dante?" I asked, cheeks feeling warm.

"*Sim*. Trust the Costa's," he said.

"What about Luca?" I asked, glancing at the front of the store. The sun was cutting through the store, creating a peaceful glow.

"Those boys are like my grandsons. You can trust them but don't feel afraid to put them in their place," he huffed. I bit back a laugh.

"I haven't so far," I said. My *avô* chuckled and I felt myself relax. Someone called to him from the other side.

"I promise to tell you everything once I'm back. Remember you are a Silva. *Beijinhos*."

The phone clicked. It was time to think. My family had been working with the mafia since I was little. So something happened. Also the shop was under neutral territory. I doubt it was because every mafia preferred my *avô*'s work.

He also didn't seem afraid of the mafias although we had to be careful on the phone. There was more to this puzzle. There was also some sort of special agreement between us and the Costa's.

The door dinged and I made my way back to the front of the shop. The devil stood before me to pick up his suit. He had a garment bag in one hand. I eyed it curiously.

"How do you feel?" he asked. He scanned my face. His eyes were filled with concern.

"A little drowsy but definitely better. Thanks again for the soup," I said. I moved to hand him his suit.

After this there was no reason for us to hang around. Our professional agreement ended here with a simple transaction of a suit. But I still had questions to ask him. He took his suit from me and handed me the bag he walked in with.

"Tonight. The charity event. You. In this dress. I'll pick you up at your apartment at seven," he said. It was a demand, not a request. A tiny thrill went down my spine. I eyed the bag.

Tonight. Tonight I would ask Dante everything.

"Seven."

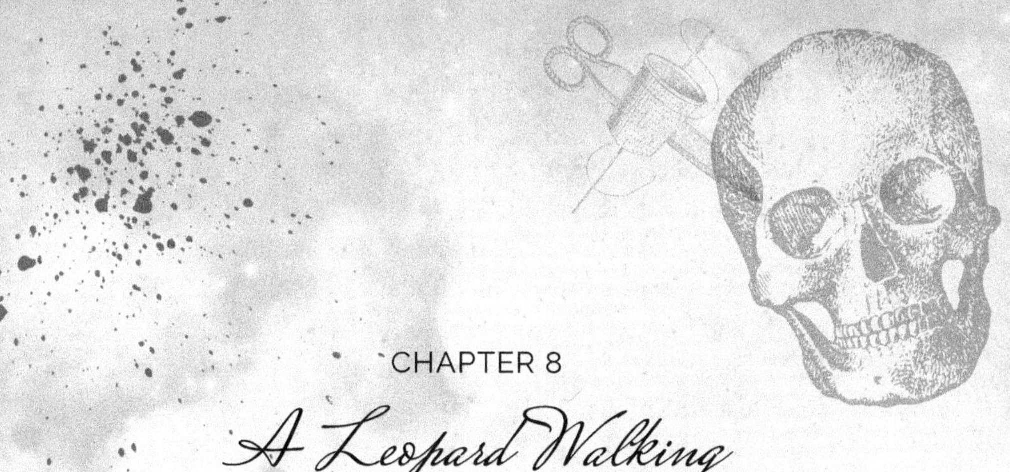

CHAPTER 8

A Leopard Walking

THERE ARE MORE MONSTERS HIDDEN IN THE SHADOWS THAN YOU KNOW MIGHT NEED TO BRING A FLASHLIGHT

I was a bundle of nerves the rest of the day. I kept eyeing the garment bag. Inside was a red backless dress that could cling to my curves. It was about to be five when I closed up shop and headed back to my apartment.

It was almost seven when I placed the last finishing touches. One thing about me is that I will always be on time no matter what. My family had always been a stickler when it came to time.

I stared at myself in the mirror. My dark hair was swept up in a loose messy bun with a few front pieces. My brown eyes were traced with black and my lips were red. Tonight I was going to get under Dante's skin and find out how much blood was on my *avô's* hands. There was a knock at the door.

"Lucia?" Dante's voice carried through the door. Taking a deep breath I walked out to open it.

Dante stood before me in the suit I made him and it made my body ache. It fit him perfectly, curving with his muscles. His dark hair was gelled back and his scruff was trimmed, accentuating his sharp cheekbones.

I was used to seeing people wear my clothes. But to see Dante? It made me want to get on my knees for him. He was wearing my name on his back and fuck that did more things to me than I thought it would. It made him feel as if he belonged to *me*.

His eyes followed the curve of my body, devouring me like I was a four course meal. I hoped I would be by the end of the night. He licked his bottom lip and handed me a single rose.

"*Bella.* I knew you would look good in that dress." His tone was oozing confidence causing me to roll my eyes.

"Mhmm. Nice suit," I said, smirking. He let out a chuckle. I felt a surge of pride. I made Dante look damn good. I couldn't help but admire my work.

"Don't look at me like that. We'll have time for that later," he teased, taking a step forward until our chests were touching. My nipples tightened and from the way his jaw tick I knew he could see. I gingerly placed my hand on his chest. His hand grazed the exposed part of my back, leaving tinges in their wake.

"We'll find out how I look out of this dress later," I promised. I pushed away to place the rose inside.

HE LED me to a black car with tinted windows. Opening the door I slid across the leather seats. A partition separated us from the driver. I could feel Dante's warmth as he slid next to me.

We drove in silence and nerves began settling across my skin. I was worried because of Dante. I knew that stepping out with him in front of all those people could mean different possibilities. And whether I wanted to, I needed to be there because I was representing my *avô's* shop. I was representing the Silva family.

I began fidgeting with my nails. Dante pulled my hands apart. "What's wrong?" he asked. His gray eyes held me still. I stared at him silently, trying to find the right words. "If it makes you feel better we can enter separately," he offered with a lopsided grin. A sigh escaped me.

"Don't worry. I get it. We'll drop you off first. Circle twice and I'll see you inside," he said. I wrapped my hand around his and squeezed. It was unnerving in the best way that he was able to read me. If we entered separately there would be less questions and I had enough on my plate to deal with. He leaned towards my ear.

"And then after we can go back to your place," he said in a hushed voice. I turned to face him with a foxy smile.

"Only if we pick up fast food on the way back," I said. He chuckled but I was serious. I didn't have the taste buds for fancy food at events like these. "I know what they serve at these flamboyant events and I don't have the palette of a silver spoon brat," I said with full confidence that made Dante laugh some more.

"I couldn't agree more," he said with an easy smile and I pulled my hand away from his, breaking the connection. Dante sat back, his smile turning into amusement. "You know what sucks?" he said. I raised an eyebrow for him to continue whatever ridiculous perverted thought he was thinking.

"That thing there," he said, pointing to the partition and my body responded. My heart picked up its pace. He leaned to place a soft kiss on my neck, causing my body to shiver. His finger traced down my bare arm. "It sucks they don't block out noise." He continued to kiss up and down my neck, coaxing faint moans.

"Are you generally loud?" I murmured. I placed a hand on his knee and began tracing circles. His eyes shot to me with hunger.

"You know I can think of a way where you won't mess up your make-up." His lips were so close. His hand rested high up on my thigh, pinching the soft fabric of my dress. I leaned slightly forward.

"But then you'll mess up my hair," I countered. His eyes spark with challenge.

"How? Can't keep still if I finger fuck you," he teased as his hand began dragging the skirt of my dress up. I sucked in a breath and my greedy hips moved, trying to ease the pressure between my thighs.

I cupped his cock through his pants and offered a squeeze. He hardened beneath my touch. His eyes fluttered close as he took a deep breath.

"You're playing rough Cinderella," he said, leaning away. His fingers traced circles at the apex of my thighs.

"And you're not doing the same?" I said, rubbing slowly.

"I like being in charge," he said, eyes closing briefly as my fingers worked him through his pants.

"And I do too," I said, nonchalantly.

"You know who I am," he said sternly. When he opened his eyes they burned. I lifted my skirt and shifted to straddle him. Dante bit his lip to keep from moaning as I rocked. My satin panties provided little barrier.

"My hair and makeup is safe now," I said with a smirk. He gripped my hips, letting me take control of the rhythm. "Just because you're in charge of other people doesn't mean you get to boss me around," I said. One of his hands slid underneath my skirt.

"Lucia," he whispered against my neck as I rocked faster. His fingers dug into my ass cheek.

"You said until I finish right? I can finish right now," I said, grinding into him. A storm of pleasure was barreling through me. Dante cursed under his breath. His hands gripped my hips again, rocking with me.

"I never said you were going to finish in the car," he hissed. I peeked at him from beneath my lashes.

"You never really declared the rules in our little game, Dante," I said, breathlessly. The car was slowing down but I was so close. I shut my eyes, enjoying the ride. My orgasm was just out of reach.

Before I could succumb to the explosion of pleasure Dante pulled me off his lap. He was breathing heavily as he adjusted himself. I bashfully watched him.

"You're right I haven't," he said, moving to grip my jaw. I clamped my hand around his wrist and our eyes clashed, fighting for dominance. "You will finish with either my mouth, my tongue or my cock," he stated. I finally pulled free from his grip to adjust the skirt of my dress. I reached for my clutch as the car rolled to a complete stop.

"I could have; on your cock just now," I said, eyeing his pants. Fuck, I couldn't wait for him to be inside me. Dante's grin was one that promised blissful torture.

"Oh Cinderella, when you come it won't be in the back of a car but on a bed where you can scream my name," he said. I reached for the handle.

"That's if you can make me scream," I said with a mischievous grin.

I was challenging him on purpose. I needed to push him so when the time came he wouldn't resist answering my questions.

"You should know I always get what I want," he said, looking determined.

"This is about getting what I want, remember?" I teased. And with that I stepped out of the car and walked into flashing lights with a painted smile.

TIME HAD PASSED and I was slowly feeling the effects of mindless conversations. I was speaking with clients and possible future clients. Many of the people here were wearing gowns we had either created or altered. I felt pride seeing that the Silva mark was glittered around the room.

I turned around to meet the eyes of a man in a deep violet suit. He took a sip of his champagne before walking up to me. A shiver crawled up my spine. There was something about this man. He stalked towards me like a leopard; dark and deadly. I swallowed.

"Ah, you're from the Silva family, correct?" he asked in a deep voice. My lungs tightened. There was something about the wicked gleam in his eyes that he was trying to mask that made my stomach twist. I tortured my face into a pleasant smile.

"Yes and you?" I said, offering a handshake. He didn't take it and that made my eyes twitch. *Rude*. Did he think I wasn't worth something as simple as a handshake?

"My name is Cole. Cole Anders," he said. The name loosely sounded familiar but I couldn't place it. The Anders for sure hadn't stepped foot inside my *avô's* shop.

"Well it's nice to meet you," I said. Although I offered politeness, all I wanted was to leave. He made me uneasy and I learned long ago to trust my gut. Although my gut also told me to not be afraid of Dante despite his career choice.

Glancing to the side I noticed Luca looking at me, jaw clenched and his hands in fists. That bad feeling in my stomach began spreading.

If sunshine Luca didn't look happy about this man talking to me that meant something. And I was once again the person with the missing puzzle pieces.

"Is there something you want?" I said, pulling my hand away. He took a step forward and I stood my ground. I needed to show him he couldn't intimidate me.

"What I want is many but I don't *want* anything from you. More like…a need," he said, casually. I took a cautious sip of my drink. I kept my eyes on him. He seemed almost amused.

"I'm a seamstress," I said, keeping my tone flat.

"Just that?" he asked. A flare of anger arose. I didn't like what he was implying. His eyes widened slightly for a second, a flash of regret. "That was rude. My apologies. I would like a suit made personally by you," he said. I eyed him as he tried to offer a genuine smile. From behind I noticed Dante walking up, his face deadly. I pulled a card from my clutch.

"It has the address and hours for the shop," I said. He took it, his fingers brushing against mine and his hand trembled slightly.

Interesting.

"But what if I require time outside the hours. I tend to be busy," he said. I nodded in understanding. I could see through his façade.

Judging from Luca's reaction and the way Dante was walking towards us this man must be one of *them*. He belonged to one of the mafia factions. He's also probably been watching my shop—watching me. I took a deep breath.

"Those are the hours Mr. Anders," I said firmly. Before he could speak again Dante interrupted.

"I was hoping for a dance Ms. Silva." Dante's voice had a hard edge.

"Mr. Costa!" Mr. Anders said with fake enthusiasm.

"Anders," Dante said quickly. The men held an internal battle through their eyes, waiting for someone to give in. Mr. Anders' gaze slid to mine again.

"We'll be in touch," Mr. Anders said, bowing slightly. Dante didn't look away until the man was out of sight. Without warning he grabbed my glass and placed it on the tray of a passing waiter.

Pulling me against him, I relaxed against him. With my heels I was slightly taller than Dante. His hand on my bare back made me tingle. I let out a breath. He placed his mouth against my ear.

"I don't want you alone with him," he whispered. We began swaying to the music.

"Trust me I don't want to be," I whispered.

Mr. Anders felt wrong. I could still feel him. It was like his energy had latched onto mine. As much as he scared me there was also a part of me that felt sad for him. But I couldn't explain why.

"Another hour and we'll head out. Still up for food?" Dante asked. I nodded. But with the way his fingers lazily traced circles on my back that wasn't all I was in the mood for.

GRABBING the food was quick and I couldn't wait to dive into the delicious greasiness. Once at my apartment we sat at the table and enjoyed the comfort of quietness, wine and burgers.

"So much better than what they had," I said while taking a bite of fries.

"The bruschetta wasn't too bad," he commented. I let out a giggle.

"Really because I saw the face you and Luca made," I pointed out. Dante shrugged his shoulders as he wiped his face.

"I wasn't in charge so who am I to judge," he said. I threw my head back in laughter.

"Really? Because I distinctly remember you questioning my degree with your judgey attitude," I said.

"Well Cinderella I can assure you that you proved me wrong," he said. Dante shot me a smile that relaxed his features. He truly was handsome. It wasn't right for a man of his nature to be that good looking.

A strong jaw that begged to be under my tongue, full lips that deserve to be nipped, stubble that's short enough to make my thighs red, a face that would make the perfect seat to make me scream.

As if he knew what I was thinking, his eyes met mine from above his wine glass. He took a slow sip and I watched as his throat bobbed up and down. I reached for my own glass feeling parched in so many ways.

Tonight was going to be my night.

ONCE WE WERE DONE EATING I moved to wipe the table. I could hear Dante's footsteps behind me. He slowly walked up from behind and placed his hands on either side of me, caging me in. I sucked in a breath. His body felt *so* good and his clothes teased my exposed skin.

"So shall we resume our game?" he asked. His breath was hot on my neck. I squared my shoulders to allow room for me to twist around. I wrapped my arms around his neck, resting my weight against the table. Dante's eyes were playful. I offered a flirtatious smile.

"Last time I checked I was winning," I said. He chuckled and grazed his lips across my cheek.

"I think that's the point, right?" he said. I hummed in agreement as he placed kisses down my neck. He gently grabbed the back of my head, gliding his fingers in between my hair, tugging my bun loose. I moaned as his fingernails scraped my scalp.

He smirked into the side of my neck. His other hand skimmed my hip, over and over again. I leaned my neck away, begging to feel his lips more. Without thinking I began unbuttoning his shirt, itching to feel his skin.

"Lucia," he muttered. His skin was hot to the touch and I scratched down his chest causing him to hiss.

"Dante?" I asked innocently. He pulled back, pressing his forehead against mine. Our bodies trembled with anticipation.

"Sì, *amore*?" he said. My heart thumped against my chest.

"Beija-me," I asked, hoping he understood what I said.

His lips tentatively touched mine, savoring, memorizing the feel. It was almost like we were melting into each other. He nipped my bottom lip and my body tightened under his hands. I slipped my hands under the back of his shirt to pull him closer. He groaned deep in his throat as our tongues slipped around each other.

The fire between us ascended until Dante couldn't take it. He pushed away roughly and tossed his shirt to the floor. I gasped and shoved him away to grab it.

"This is Tim Forn. You are not leaving this on the floor," I chastised. I placed it around the back of one of the chairs. Something hard pressed against my ass causing me to grip the edge of the table. He kissed down the back of my neck and over my shoulder blades while his fingers toyed with the zipper at my lower back.

"This isn't a bad position," he mumbled. I leaned forward to push against him, needing more friction. "Fuck," he hissed. I giggled. I knew what I was doing and liked having the upper hand. He grabbed my hips, pushing forward roughly and I gasped as I collapsed on top of the table. I leaned back against him, arching my back. This felt too good.

I glanced over my shoulder to see a shirtless Dante, breathing heavy. His hair had tumbled forward, across his eyes. He was becoming undone and it was breathtaking. He glanced at my dress.

"May I take the dress off?" he asked, giving a coy smile. His fingers slipped under my straps. I stood up, pulling away from him. I strutted towards the bedroom, slowly unzipping my dress. Once at the door I looked over my shoulder again. Dante's hands trembled, itching to touch me again. I gave him a wink.

"Play your cards right and you might win too, Dante," I said and then my dress dropped to the floor.

CHAPTER 9

Bedroom Interrogation

THERE ARE MANY SECRETS LURKING BEHIND CLOSED DOORS TIME TO BUST THAT SHIT OPEN.

I sat on the edge of the bed waiting for Dante. My heart was pounding against my chest. I was throwing all caution to the wind but I didn't give a flying fuck.

Tonight was about me. I would get more answers from Dante but that didn't mean I couldn't enjoy myself in the process.

He leaned against the doorway in admiration. His eyes were dark with desire and the shadows from the living room light painted him as a dark angel. He walked over, standing in front of me. I raised an eyebrow. He offered his hand. I took it, allowing him to pull me up. We both sighed in delight as our skins pressed against each other.

His hands slid up and down my body, feeling the parts that curved and dipped. He placed a soft kiss on my bare shoulder, making his way up.

"So soft," he whispered against my neck

"Lotion," I said absentmindedly. He chuckled. My hands began to dig into his skin. "It's very important. You probably use it with all chemicals you have to use when-" I froze. He cupped my face and looked into my eyes. I knew what he could see. He saw the trickle of fear in them. He saw the remembrance of what stood between us.

His lips crashed against mine. He kissed me hard as if trying to erase

78

the thoughts. He bit down on my lip roughly, tugging. I gasped and Dante took that as an opportunity.

The second our tongues touched my body gave away slightly. He held me against him. His fingers grazed down my back with a pressure that made me shiver. It was rough, the way I secretly craved.

"Lay back, *ora*," he said, pushing me back. He placed one knee on the edge of the bed. He lifted my right foot and began to massage. "You were in heels for a while," he said.

I pressed the side of my face into the bed, trying not to squirm. I opened my legs wider for him. His eyes traveled down with hunger. He worked his way up my calf, changing the pressure as he watched my reaction.

"I've also caused you a lot of stress the past few days," he said, keeping his voice soft. He stopped at my knee to switch legs. He was being attentive. It bewildered me how a man could be as ferocious as a wolf and also gentle like a swan.

"Tonight I want you to let me show you how much I admire your work, your strength and beauty," he said, whispering the sweetness against my skin. I mewled at his worship of me.

"You can go harder," I pleaded. He hummed in approval.

"Not yet, Cinderella," he said. I groaned and reached for him but he pulled my hands over my head. He was careful to keep his body from touching mine.

"Let me," he urged. I rolled my eyes. "You don't need to be in control, Lucia," he said. I squirmed as he kissed my cheek. He slipped his arm under my shoulders, pushing me further up the bed. My eyes widen at his surge of strength.

"I'm going to finish massaging your legs," he stated. He grabbed my right leg and hooked it over his shoulder. I bucked my hips, needing his fingers or his mouth on my cunt. With all the slow touches I was getting wet and it wasn't enough. His eyes trailed over, excited.

The second he began kneading my thigh I moaned. His hands made their way slowly to the top of my thigh. He was close to where I needed him to be. My clit was throbbing. My breathing was becoming erratic with anticipation. But instead of giving me what I wanted he switched legs.

"Should I put my leg down?" I asked, looking at him, brows furrowed.

"I need your legs in this position for when I'm done massaging," he said with a devilish grin. I licked my lips.

"Well, get to it," I said. He gave a dark chuckle, his hands working my body.

"Should I take my time?" he teased. I snaked my hand through his hair and tugged, forcing him to meet my gaze.

"Does it look like you should?" I said. His eyes went back to my pussy. He pressed his nose, inhaling my scent and I arched at the feel. He groaned, deep in his throat. He spared me one more glance before I felt his tongue in between my lips. I gasped as he quickly found my clit.

I tugged him hard as he began sucking. My entire body ignited as Dante devoured me like I was his last meal. One arm snaked around my hips, lifting me up. My legs squeeze around his head as his tongue teased my hole. I mewled as his tongue dipped in. This wasn't enough though. His tongue curved around my clit, made its way back down to my hole and then up again.

"More," I cried out. He slipped two fingers inside easily, stretching me and began taking long languid strokes against my sensitive bud of nerves. I clamped around his fingers and rocked against his hand.

But it still wasn't enough. I lowered my hands to squeeze my own breasts. I played with my nipples, pulling them until they were hard pebbles. Dante watched me play with myself, his strokes growing harder. The noises coming out of my body were driving me higher. He added another finger as he bit the inside of my thigh. I gasped.

"I gotta stretch you, *amore*," he whispered against the bruised skin. His fingers scissored, stretching me, filling me. I rocked with him as he sucked my clit. I fought between suffocating him with my legs and widening to give him more room.

The air around us tightened as I struggled to breathe. Everything felt overwhelming and yet not enough. I still needed more. Dante's fingers sped up and I began crying out his name. A warmth was emerging in my lower belly, a sign of my impending orgasm. I think Dante must have sensed it because he pulled out. I glared at him. His lips glistened with my taste. Dante sucked his fingers clean of my arousal and I pulled him in for a rough kiss, tasting myself on his tongue. Dante groaned as I shoved him away.

I pointed to the drawer and he silently followed my instructions. I watched him as he carefully took off his pants, folded them and placed them on my dresser.

"Good boy. Can't mess up those pants. They were expensive," I said, still teasing my nipples. Dante grunted as he rolled the condom onto his cock. It wasn't too long but it had girth. It was going to feel fucking great.

He made it onto the bed and I reached for his shoulders. We needed to do this fast before my brain caught up with me. I sat up and pushed him on his back. He listened, lying back. I straddle him, rubbing my pussy against his dick, getting it wet. His hands shot to my hips and he cursed.

"Fuck, *Bella*," he hissed as I took his cock in my hands and rolled my hips against the head of his cock. I took a deep breath as I slowly lowered myself. My head fell back in bliss, feeling him stretch me to the point of burning. Dante began rocking my hips to help ease himself inside. My hands landed on his chest as I gasped. He felt too fucking good.

"Yes," I hissed. Dante unexpectedly sat up causing us to rock and I whimpered as I felt him fully inside of me. He pulled my nipple into his mouth and I smiled. My fingers tugged at his hair as I rocked fast against him. My orgasm was building back up again. Dante snaked his hand down to rub my clit. My body began wounding tighter and tighter.

"You're choking my cock and it feels *so* fucking good," he said, pressing his forehead against mine. I wrapped my hands around his neck, needing leverage. "Fuck me, Lucia. Fuck me hard."

"I'll fuck you how I want. So be a good boy and keep playing with my nipples," I said, smirking. Dante's eyes sparked and like a good mafia man he listened. Taking my other nipple in his mouth, his tongue flicked back and forth as he pinched the other with his hand. I gasped at the overstimulation.

At first I rocked back and forth, needing more friction. But the longer I went the more I just *needed*. My thighs burned as I switched motions. The feeling of my chest bouncing against his added a wave of new sensations.

I kept my eyes on him as I began to bounce uncontrollably, all sense of rhythm lost to this delicious sensation. His name tumbled out of me over and over again. I begged and pleaded for him.

"Dante?" My voice came out as a whimper. He nodded. "Slap my ass," I demanded. I felt myself building up higher and higher until Dante slapped his hand across my ass and I exploded.

Before I could recover his hands gripped my hips, taking over, treating me like a doll and I let him. I let him chase his own orgasm as he chased the remnants of mine away.

And just when I thought I was done another orgasm slammed into me as he finished. My fingers created half moons along his shoulders and I smiled. He looked amazingly marked by me. We stayed in each other's arms for a few minutes, catching our breath.

Once he became soft, Dante lifted me up and pulled out slowly. I hissed at the loss. He laid me down and kissed the center of my chest.

"Wait here," he said.

A few minutes later he came back with a wet warm towel to wipe me. I let him take care of me. I let him clean me up as he continued to compliment my mind and my body.

I headed to the bathroom to pee once he finished. I stared at the mirror; taking note of my wild appearance. My hair was like a bird's nest. My makeup was smudged, lipstick wiped off. Across my neck and down my chest were red marks. A few of them would most likely turn into bruises.

I smiled. I wouldn't mind that. We marked each other. And while I felt I now owned a part of Dante I was beginning to think that maybe he owned a part of me as well. I took one more glance at the mirror and nodded.

It was time for questions.

DANTE WAS LYING in my bed in his briefs, scrolling through his phone. I guess the life of a mafia man never ends, not even after amazing sex.

I strolled into my room, naked with a clean face. His eyes followed me as I placed an oversize shirt and got into bed. Dante placed his hands underneath the shirt, stroking the top of my thighs once I sat next to him.

"That was amazing," he murmured into my neck. I smiled. While I was satisfied I couldn't help but feel anxious. I exposed my neck to give him more room and he took it. I glanced up at my ceiling. It was now or never. I slid my fingers into his hair and pulled. He eyed me curiously.

"I have questions," I said. Dante smirked. His hands traveled up my thighs to my breasts, cupping each.

"Mhmm. I was wondering when your interrogation was going to begin," he said as he began kneading my breasts. My clit throbbed with need again. I pushed to straddle him. Dante sighed. He gripped my hips and moved me until I was sitting on his cock again.

"So you knew," I said, rocking slightly. His eyes closed briefly and he hummed in acknowledgement.

"I've just been waiting for you to ask," he said. His hands stay on my hips.

"Would you like to begin the interrogation this way or in a more respectable manner?" I asked. Was I using this moment for selfish reasons? Yes. But I was giving him an out.

Dante lifted my shirt until I was naked on top of him. I lifted my hips and he tugged his briefs off. I guess there was no point in putting on clothes in the first place. He placed his hands on the back of his head, shifting to get comfortable.

"I prefer this way, *amore*," he said with a grin. I shrugged my shoulders. I felt his dick begin to harden against me. His body tensed slightly as I continued my slow rock. My thighs were still burning from having sex but I could feel myself growing wet again.

"What kind of agreement does my *avô* have?" I asked. Dante's jaw tick.

"He makes suits for the mafias. His area is neutral ground, no fighting," he said with a grunt. I rocked slightly harder against him and Dante bucked his hip. A soft moan escaped my lips.

"Why?" I managed to get out. He raised an eyebrow. I shook my head. I could already feel myself giving into my desires. I needed to focus but the feel of Dante under me was intoxicating. "Why is his land neutral I mean? There must be a reason," I said. Dante's hands rocked me harder as my hands dug into his chest, trying to hold myself up.

"That's something your grandfather should tell you," he said. I groaned in frustration.

"Mr. Anders is in the mafia?" I asked. He had to be. His whole presence oozed the same darkness as Dante. A bead of sweat dripped down Dante's face as his cheeks puffed. I leaned forward slightly to give my clit more friction.

"Yes. Americans. We don't like them," Dante said before pausing. He bucked his hips roughly causing me to gasp. "Fuck—they're being sketchy," he said as he tilted his head up. Another orgasm was building. The Americans? They wanted something. And Mr. Anders was curious about my shop.

Dante helped to rock me against his cock until we were both covered in sweat and his cum. Dante cursed multiple times as he stared at his stomach. I reached for his finger and ran it over his cum before sucking it into my mouth.

"You're a dream," he whispered blissfully. I leaned over, kissing him so that this time he tasted his own arousal. His hand gripped the back of my neck holding me in place. When he finally released his hold on me he looked satisfied but I had only one thought in my head.

The Americans wanted my territory.

CHAPTER 10

A Woman's Word

DON'T BE A PUPPET WHEN YOU WERE BORN TO PULL THE STRINGS

Spending the night with Dante did something to me. Something shifted inside of me. While I knew he was the devil beneath an expensive suit I didn't see him that way anymore. He went on to explain the things his people did. They helped the community where the government failed. They got things done. People treated them with respect.

But also fear. I wasn't sure how I felt about that part. Maybe his dick just did something to me. He definitely knows what he's doing with it.

I would like a suit made personally by you.

Cole Anders was a part of the American mafia. They ruled over the city of Eagle Pointe. He was a slightly tall man made of muscle. His hair was a tawny brown cut short with dark eyes.

While he gave off a dark aura there was a second where I saw something behind his eyes the night of the charity event. Something that made me sad. His people wanted my territory. Dante said that it was a possibility but I knew it was true. I felt it in my bones.

However my city was classified as neutral ground. Meaning none of the clans could fight on my turf. My stomach twisted.

How could a simple agreement from my *avô* keep these people at

85

bay? There was more to it. There had to be. But Dante refused to tell me anything. It needed to come from my *avô's* mouth.

I shook my head. I needed to get through the work day and then I was going to have a talk with my *avô*, whether he wanted to or not.

The sun was barely rising when I strolled up to my shop. The sound of glass crashing stopped me in my tracks. Up ahead was my shop. The door was swinging open widely as two masked men stood outside. Anger seared through my veins.

"What the fuck do you think you're doing?" I screamed, pulling my small taser from my bag. The men turned to me with wide eyes beneath their ski masks. I took a step forward, taser buzzing.

"I'm going to call the cops you fucking assholes," I yelled as I began running towards them

"This crazy bitch!" One of them shouted as they both sprinted down the street. I stopped in front of my shop, watching their retreating figures. My heart sank.

The door was busted open and inside racks were knocked over. My hands kept shaking as I fumbled for my phone. I stared at the blank screen. I should call the cops. Should I though? I bit my lip. I slipped my phone back in my pocket.

I trusted my gut and took a step inside. My shop was cold from the breeze that was pouring in from the outside. I stepped over clothes to make it to the cash register. I luckily emptied it out last night.

But my eyes widened when I could see that it remained untouched.

"That's fucking weird," I muttered. Something told me to check the office. I made my way to the back of the shop where the office door stood ajar.

Taking a deep breath I clutched my taser. I leaned towards the door. No sound. I pushed the door open as my taser crackled through the air.

The office was empty but there were papers everywhere. Every draw was open and scattered on the floor. The chair was knocked over. Those fuckers. My heart raced and I stared at my phone again, my fingers automatically dialing.

"Someone tried breaking in," I said into my phone.

I WAS STILL CLEANING up the front of the store when Dante and Luca rushed in. I had kept Dante's phone number after we baked bread. He left it on a piece of paper on my coffee table.

A few of their men hung behind them. Dante looked devastatingly gorgeous in a black polo and slacks while Luca wore a white dress shirt tucked into navy blue pants. I crossed my arms.

"Took you boys long enough," I said glaring at them. Luca stepped forward and cradled my elbows. His blue eyes bled with concern.

"Are you okay?" he asked. I snorted.

"Yeah but those fuckers were two seconds away from being burnt to crisp by my taser," I said. Luca placed a kiss on my forehead and my eyes cut to Dante. I couldn't tell if he was okay with Luca's affection or not.

"Doesn't seem like too much damage," Dante pointed out. He snapped his fingers at his men who stood awaiting orders. "Help her clean this up."

"Please," I added, eyeing Dante. He rolled his eyes.

"Please," Dante said. The men did their best to suppress their chuckle. Luca stepped away and Dante cupped my cheek.

"You okay?" he asked. I looked between him and Luca.

"I'm fine guys," I said. And I was. Because I wasn't scared of the two men that broke into my *avô's* shop. Sure I had adrenaline pumping through me when I saw them. But it wasn't because I was scared. It was because I was pissed off.

"Did they take anything? We can get it replaced," Luca offered. I motioned for them to follow me to the office. They glanced at each other before looking at me and following. Once inside the office I waved at Dante to close the door.

"Fuck, this place is even more trashed," Dante said. I nodded, lifting the chair back up to sit at the desk. Both men stood before me, watching me, waiting. I crossed my arms over my chest.

"They weren't after money. The register was untouched and this place was more ransacked than out there where there's expensive merchandise," I pointed out. Luca's hands fidgeted at his sides. He quickly glanced at Dante. Dante's nostrils flared.

Well, well, well. These boys thought they could hide something from me. All the men in my life apparently did. But they underestimated me. They underestimate my ability to read into situations. You learn quickly when you live in a world run by men.

"Those men didn't want a fucking three piece suit. They were looking for something," I said. I propped my feet on the desk. "Someone better fucking tell me about this agreement my *avô* has because I can sure as hell tell this isn't some simple neutral territory bullshit."

AFTER CLEANING up the office they forced me to go back to my apartment while they went on mafia business. I sat on my couch annoyed as shit. Who the fuck would dare fuck with my shop? Who thought that was a brilliant idea? If they thought that would scare me they had another thing coming.

There was a swift knock at my door. "Luca?" I said, letting him in. He smiled down at me and stepped inside. "What's up?"

Luca walked into my apartment as if he lived here. He was completely at peace removing his shoes and making his way to my couch.

"Dante is securing a meeting with some of our people," he said. He ran a hand through his blonde hair and my eyes stared at the way his bicep bulged. Luca was a model pretty boy handsome. And for some reason I couldn't help but stare at him. I took a seat across from him.

"Why?" I asked, curiously.

"We both know that wasn't a simple break in," he pointed out. I crossed my arms over my chest. His eyes flickered down briefly and I blushed. At this point I was used to Luca's flirtatious way. I chalked it up to his personality. He scooted himself closer and took my hand in his.

"We're going to figure this out and I promise everything will make sense to you soon," he said, softly. My body relaxed, leaning towards him. Dante provided fire that made me feel powerful and Luca calmed me, allowing me to let go.

He wrapped his arms around me and I leaned my head against his chest. His heartbeat was steady and sure like his words. His hands traced lines up and down my back, luring my eyes closed. He was so warm. I found myself pressing against him more.

"Lucia?" Luca's voice was soft. I hummed, looking up at him. His blue eyes were bright and they wandered all over my face drinking me in. "May I kiss you?" he asked, cupping my cheek. My eyes widened and my core clenched.

"Um. The thing is Dante…" I began to say but his smirk made me pause. His hand slowly trailed down my face towards my neck.

"What makes you think he would be upset?" he asked. I bit my lip. From the brief conversations I've had with both of them in the room, a part of me secretly thought that something like this could be a possibility. But I didn't want to assume. They were cousins after all and the last thing I wanted was two men fighting over me. Especially men with the ability to kill.

"Aren't mafia men possessive?" I asked. Luca shifted me onto his lap and my eyes fluttered briefly closed. He felt good under me too. Where Dante was shorter and more broad, Luca was long and lean. His hands slipped under my shirt, resting at my hips. He trailed his nose across my cheek before taking a nip at my earlobe. I bit back a gasp.

"Mhmm but some of us like to share," he said. I swallowed a moan as his fingers teased the hemline of my leggings.

"Are you sure he wouldn't mind if I have a taste of you?" I asked, pulling back. My heart hammered in my chest. I had never been in this kind of predicament. Hell I hadn't been on a date let alone slept with a guy for two years and now I had two men at my feet.

"I'll give you more than a taste," he said with a grin. Luca shifted and pulled his phone out of his pocket. He scrolled through it before handing me his phone. It was a text exchange from today when we were cleaning up the office together.

DADDY DON DANTE

After Lucia goes back to her apartment I need
you to stay with her while I assemble a meeting

Oooo you're going to let me be alone with her
in her apartment. Aren't you a sweetie?

Don't roll your eyes at me.

I'm rolling them because you're an idiot who
calls me sweetie. Just make sure she's okay.

I might kiss her if you leave us alone

You kiss her if she says yes to that dipshit. We
may be criminals but we ask for consent

Oooo Daddy Don talking about consent gets
me hard

Shut the fuck up and take care of our woman.

Our woman.

Our.

I stared into Luca's blue eyes. They talked about me. They talked
about having me, sharing me. My panties grew wet and I began to rock
myself on Luca. I dropped the phone and he took the hint, cradling my
head. I leaned forward and before our lips could touch Luca pulled me
away.

"No, no *gattina*. Daddy Don said I needed consent. So be a good girl
and give me what I want," he said. My hands dug into his chest. Fuck. I
did not expect that from Luca. With Dante, yes.

Well, after my night with Dante it was easy to understand that while
to the outside world he was the boss, behind closed doors I had the reins.

Luca gripped my hips, lifting me up before roughly pulling me down
against his erection. I cried out, my head falling back. With his hand still
on my neck, he brought me forward and dug his teeth into the bruise
Dante had left.

"*Gattina*," he said with a singsong voice. He shoved my body flushed
against his and cocked his head waiting. "Just because Dante is patient

doesn't mean I am. Do not think we are the same," he said with a wicked grin. *Fuck it.*

"Kiss m-," the words were barely out of my mouth when he crushed his lips against mine. Luca was right. He was nothing like Dante.

With Dante I had one hand on the wheel but with Luca I wasn't in charge. He bit into my bottom lip so hard that I gasped. He took the opportunity to coax my tongue out. His hands wandered down, roughly touching me. He sucked my tongue into his mouth and my body lit up. I threw my hands into his hair, tugging. We were nothing but tongues and teeth, fighting for control.

I rocked faster against him, needing to come. His mouth made its way to the back of my neck, biting and licking next to the bruises that Dante had left. He was leaving his marks next to Dante. I slipped my hands under his dress shirt, creating half-moons into his shoulders with my nails.

A phone beeped and Luca pulled away from me to check. I bit back a snarky remark when I noticed Luca's reaction. He tossed his phone to the coffee table.

A calloused hand roughly grabbed my jaw, forcing me to look into his eyes. "Listen to me. We have to leave in about ten minutes so I'm going to fuck you hard and fast," he said, his voice dripping with lust. I swallowed hard. *This man.*

He gripped the back of my thighs and stood up. I wrapped my legs around him quickly. He walked over to my kitchen counter, his erection rubbing over me. I moaned loudly.

Once I was spread out on the counter, Luca tugged down my leggings and underwear. I heard the faint unbuckling of a belt. Luca's pants and briefs were hanging low enough to let his cock out. My mouth hung open, hungry and a little nervous. Luca didn't have the same girth as Dante but he was longer. My core clenched emptiness, needing to be filled. Before I could reach for him his hand smacked my aching pussy. I moaned again.

"I'm going to fuck this pussy, Lucia," Luca promised as he ripped open a condom. I pulled my shirt up, exposing my breasts as he sheathed himself. "Hold the counter," he demanded. The second my hands had touched the counter's edge behind me Luca thrusted into me in one motion. My shrieks quickly turned into moans with every rock of Luca's glorious cock. I hitched my legs higher up on his waist, locking my ankles.

Luca leaned over me, our mouths fusing against each other as he continued to rut into me. "Five minutes," he said as his hand traced circles around my clit. I clenched around him as the familiar warm feeling shot through my body.

With a few strokes and flick of my clit I screamed Luca's name as electricity sparked through me. Luca's pace turned unhinged as he chased his orgasm and I smacked his thigh to urge him on.

"So fucking tight and p-perfect," he groaned as my nails dug into his ass. I did my best to tilt my hips up, the angle changing to the point where Luca's body dropped against mine. "Baby you're choking me so good. Give me another," he said, pressing a kiss to my breast. I nodded, too weak to argue.

Luca lifted up and held my waist off the counter as I twisted and pulled at my nipples. His pupils were blown wide enough I couldn't quite see the blue. His blonde hair has fallen forward. Right now, with his cock thrusting inside of me and my legs wrapped around his waist he looked like a demented Italian god.

His finger swiped around my clit and his thrust turned hard and deep. I nodded back and forth pleading for more. It didn't take much to make me cry out his name again and Luca groaned deep in his throat. He laid me back on the counter and pulled out slowly.

I was still a mess on the counter, trying to catch my breath when Luca cleaned me up. He ran a hand through his hand and adjusted his shirt. He looked as if he didn't just have amazing sex while I was still half naked on my kitchen counter.

There was a soft click at my door and footsteps. I reached to yank my shirt down but Luca stopped me with a smirk.

Dante.

Dante stood in my living room and my eyes went back and forth between both men. His gray eyes traveled over my pussy that was still on display before glancing at his cousin with a smirk.

"How do you feel, *Bella*?" Dante asked. I blink slowly. My whole body is hot watching both of these men stare at me with hunger.

"Throughly fucked," I managed to say. Dante nodded, placing a hand on his cousin's shoulder.

"Good. Now let's go. We have a meeting."

I WAS PULLING up to an extravagant house in the suburbs. Specifically in Costa territory. Luca and Dante told me we would be meeting with his men to discuss the break in. But anything concerning 'the agreement' was strictly for my *avô* to talk about. His men had spent the afternoon installing cameras in my shop which I was grateful for.

I was walking across shiny tile floors and being escorted into a room with a giant wooden table and chairs. The men sitting at the chairs eyed me. Some I recognized as customers and others I didn't. But what was obvious was that I was not welcomed.

I walked in between Dante and Luca. I straighten my back, not giving the men a second to doubt me. Dante pulled a seat open near the front and offered me to sit. Luca sat across from me next to an older gentleman who had the same gray eyes as Dante. Dante himself, sat at the head of the table.

"Dante, why are we here?" a man asked. Dante glanced at the man who I assumed was his father before speaking.

"Silva's shop was broken into," Dante stated. Someone let out a dry cough and my eyes trailed to find the culprit.

"And? Break-ins happen all the time," someone said. I snorted. Everyone's eyes turned to me.

"Who is she?" someone said with an annoyed tone. I swirled my chair to face an old man with a receding hairline.

"Lucia Maria Silva," I stated firmly. There was no way in hell I was going to let any of them intimidate me. Whispers broke out around us.

"And what? You want us to catch the thieves who stole from your little shop?" someone said with a chuckle. I dug my fingers into my knees.

This is why I had a temper. Because men like them were a piece of shit. Men like them thought very little of women and didn't realize the power we held. I pretended to pluck a hair from my sweater.

"The men weren't looking to get some suits," I said, before making eye contact with asshole number one. "They were looking for something. Something of my *avô's*. And with the way Cole Anders approached me with an interest in me and my *little* shop I think it might have to do with this little neutral territory that you men are keeping from me," I said, sitting back in my chair. Silence engulfed the room. I swore the temperature dropped.

And then I stood up and all eyes followed me. I moved to the head of the table and tapped Dante's shoulder. He scooted himself to the side allowing me space. I eyed the second asshole who called my *avô's* shop *little*.

"Oh and my little shop? Really? Because the suit you're wearing came from my shop. The same suit that you wore with your wife Marie when you both attended the charity to raise money for the private airplane hangar on the outskirts of Costa territory," I said. I leaned my hands on my table, glaring at each man.

"You can try to belittle my job and my *avô's* shop but you wear *our* clothes when you do your fucking business. You taint *our* clothes with your blood and the blood of others. Your wives, your mistresses, significant others wear *our* designs before they drop to the floor to fuck you. So you will respect what my family has provided you," I said, keeping my voice as even as possible.

The room once again was silent. The men looked away, afraid to meet my eyes. A deep chuckle rang through the air. I turned to see the old man with gray eyes.

"You sure are a Silva, Lucia," he praised. I nodded. He turned to Dante who stood up from his seat.

"You want the truth don't you? Your grandfather is on his way back to talk to you. Until then you will continue your life as normal. I assure you we will protect you in the meantime while we find out if those men were a part of the Anders clan," Dante said.

I stared at the table. My *avô* was coming home. In a few days I would have the answers I needed. But that wasn't enough. I knew I was right. Something in my gut told me. I tilted my head, staring at him. He raised an eyebrow.

"I'll find out," I said simply. Luca stood from his chair.

"Lucia-" he began before I cut him off with a wave of my hand. Some of the men standing from the back took a step forward. I glared at them. What? Did they really think I was going to do something to Luca? I was impulsive sometimes but I wasn't stupid.

"I will find out faster than you all," I said, shrugging my shoulders. Luca shook his head.

"Lucia let us handle this," Dante said.

"Why do you think you can do it faster?" Dante's father asked, intrigued. Instead of going back to my seat I took Dante's. It was a bold move and I could tell the men didn't like it. But Dante's father didn't flinch and if he didn't I figured I was safe.

"Because I have an appointment with Cole Anders for a consultation on a suit tomorrow."

CHAPTER 11

A Feast At The Table

YOU SHOULD ALWAYS BE REWARDED FOR PUTTING MEN IN THEIR PLACE

I had a feeling I should have mentioned the appointment to Luca and Dante before blurting it out to the men but I was pissed. They really thought so little of me. Granted they didn't really know me but still. I was a Silva. Dante had dismissed everyone out of the room but Luca stayed behind.

"You're not meeting with him," Luca said. I rolled my eyes, leaning back into the chair.

"I am," I stated. Dante shook his head.

"Lucia," Dante warned. I let out an exasperated sigh.

"What? It's a consultation. I'll ask him questions about the suit and figure out if he hired those two men to break into my shop," I said. Luca shoved his fingers into his hair before standing in front of me.

"The Anders are dangerous, *gattina*," Luca said. I cocked my head.

"No shit," I asked. Dante chuckled.

"She sure has the bite of one," Dante said. My face flushed and I glanced at Luca whose eyes flashed with excitement. I cleared my throat awkwardly.

"You're installing cameras in my shop," I said, standing up. I placed a hand on Luca's chest. "If you're so worried. You can watch the cameras," I said. Luca's lips twitched.

"I do like watching," Luca said, in a low voice. My heart rattled against my chest and a feeling went straight down to my core. Dante clapped a hand on Luca's shoulder.

"Fine. *We* will watch and be nearby in incase he tries anything. But promise us you'll be careful," Dante said. I nodded. Dante squeezed Luca's shoulder.

"Luca, give us a few minutes alone." Dante's voice shifted to something darker. His words dipped in a sultry way. Luca looked between us.

"But I like watching," Luca murmured. My whole body buzzed now in anticipation. Did I like the idea of Luca watching while his cousin did whatever he was thinking? Yeah. I really fucking did.

"I know you do but I want alone time," he said, shoving Luca away. Luca sighed and headed towards the door. I raised an eyebrow at Dante.

The second Luca closed the door behind him Dante bent down to lift me. I wrapped my legs around his waist, enjoying the slight stretch. He was already hard. He settled me on the table before kissing my neck. I bit my lip to keep my whimpers from spilling. Dante began sucking and biting my neck. The bruises they left were going to be darker. I knew it.

"First my kitchen counter and now a table. Starting to feel like I'm something to be eaten," I murmured. I began rocking against him. He pushed me back until I was laying down. He tugged my sweater over my head before placing a kiss at the center of my chest.

"Well you did so well Lucia. You were thrown in the middle of a wolf's den and you stood your ground," he said, leaving me to lock the door. "I think you deserve to be eaten," he said. I leaned my head back to watch him walk back towards me.

"By the big bad wolf?" I asked, raising an eyebrow. Dante came to stand in front of me.

"Every time I have a meeting here I want to be reminded of your body laid across like a *feast* for me," he said as he stepped between my legs. He unbuttoned my jeans and tugged them down to my ankles. "Every time I sign a paper I want to be reminded of the *sweet* whimpers that came out of your mouth." He pulled my panties down before kneeling. "And I especially want to be reminded of how your pussy *tastes* when I'm sitting here having a cup of coffee."

Those were his last words before he dove in. His tongue circled my clit before giving a rough lick. I gaped, arching my back against the wood. I bit my hand to keep my moans at bay. Dante's hands dug into my skin, scratching upwards. I wrapped my legs around his shoulders, shoving him against my pussy.

Dante pushed me further up the table so he could lean down comfortably. One hand cupped my breast, massaging it slowly. He looked up at me, his eyes locked onto mine. I pulled my hand out of my mouth and gasped for air.

"I don't want to complain but don't we have shit to do?" I asked. Dante replaced his tongue with his finger. His finger slowly swirled around my clit and then moved down to my entrance.

"Yes. But you basically commanded my men in front of me—in front of my father. You didn't care about the murder in their eyes for disrespecting me," he said as he grazed my nipple with his teeth. I cradled his head, arching my back. "Now let me disrespectfully worship your body," he said, taking my nipple back in his mouth.

I mewled, my legs trying to wrap around him as he sucked my nipple. His other hand grabbed my leg, spreading me out like dessert.

"You look so good spread out for me, *Bella*," he said. I nodded, rocking my hips against the air. While he tortured my breasts his hand traveled down until his finger back on my entrance. It was aching to be filled. I moaned back into my hand. I shook my head at him. He smirked.

"Do you want to come on my fingers?" he teased, only pressing the tip of two fingers inside. I scooted my ass down and the tip of his finger slipped further in. I arched an eyebrow at him. He chuckled before lowering his head again.

He thrusted his fingers inside and I closed my eyes. I could hear how wet I was as his fingers pumped in and out of me, over and over again. He was wounding me up to burst. His tongue circled my clit again.

This time he gently nipped after every few circles with his tongue. He was building me up. Dante was like a wave. Giving my body just enough to take me close to the edge and then retreating. Where Luca was hard and fast, Dante took his time. He lapped me up, devouring me. I pinched my other nipple and Dante's eyes darkened as we worked together to bring my body to climax.

"P-please," I hissed. That was all he needed. Dante pressed further into my pussy, his fingers curling, pumping faster and harder as my walls squeezed.

My legs tightened and my body vibrated as the wave crashed over and over again. I bit my hand harder. My body exploding threatened all sorts of noises to tumble out.

Dante kept pumping into me until every spasm left my body. I sagged against the table. He pulled his fingers out of me and sucked them clean. I looked at him with hazy eyes.

"If you ever need a reminder about this table, let me know," I said, trying to catch my breath.

Consulting The Enemy

THE SAYING IS KEEP YOUR FRIENDS CLOSE AND YOUR ENEMIES CLOSER BUT SOMETIMES IT'S HARD TO TELL WHICH IS WHICH

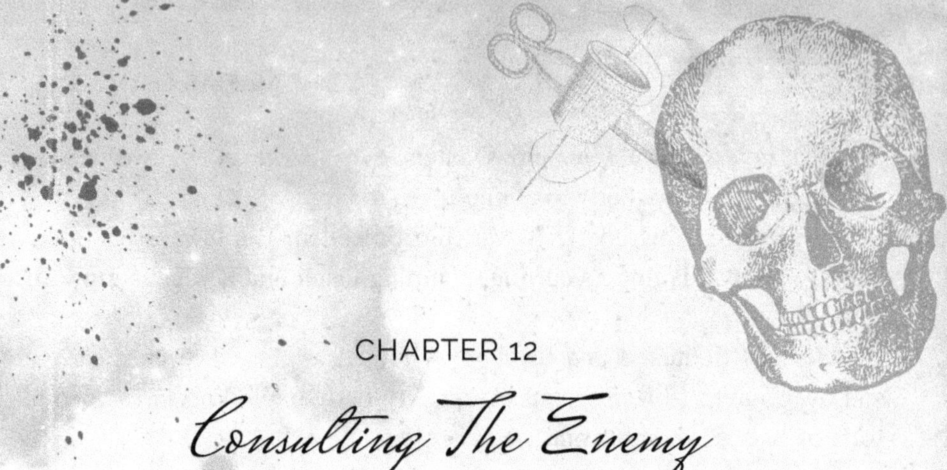

The next day the shop looked normal. You would have never suspected two men had broken in. But while I spent the day inside of the shop, sewing a few dresses, I could see Costa's men passing by the windows every once in a while. It didn't ease the growing feeling inside though.

While I was told to trust the Costa men, they weren't *my* men. They had no reason to help me nor protect me. I could only trust that they would listen to Dante.

Walking around the shop I felt like I could still feel the presence of those masked men. Their footsteps were like ghosts floating around.

My hands slightly shook as I looked at the clock. Any second Cole Anders would be strolling in for a consultation and I had to get info out of him. I needed to know how this territory factored in with the mafias.

I finished off the hem of a dark green velvet dress. I held it up in the light. It had a high neckline that was bejeweled. It sparkled in the light along with the rest of fabric that held tiny hints of glitter. It also had a high slit. I felt envious of this dress. I designed it for no one in particular. That was a lie. I designed it for me. It was going to go on a mannequin as a sample.

If people were interested in it then I would recreate it for them. I was folding it when the bells of the door rang. I sucked in a breath before turning around. It was time.

Cole Anders walked in with his hair parted to the side. His clothes were more casual this time but wreaked expensive. He had on white polo and khaki slacks. He pulled off his faux brown leather jacket. He wore a simple gold chain around his neck that I bet cost as much as this shop. I plastered on a smile.

"Mr. Anders! Good afternoon," I said, walking up to shake his hand. He eyed it for a second before giving me a firm shake. Good. I hated when people gave a weak handshake. He gave me a hesitant smile. Interesting. He had no problem at the charity ball giving me snide smiles.

But now that it was the two of us he seemed more like a prey than predator. I did remember noticing there was a flash of regret in his eyes. There was more to him. Maybe I could use that to my advantage.

"Thank you for meeting with me so quickly," he said curtly.

"Follow me this way," I said, leading him to my sewing machine. I offered him the seat across. From the corner of my eye I noticed a camera was angled at Cole's back and for some reason that's what I wanted. I wanted to watch Cole for myself. I needed to assess the situation.

"What is it that you're looking for particularly?" I asked, opening my notebook. Cole glanced around the shop before meeting my eyes.

"I would like a classic three piece suit," he said. I nodded, taking notes.

"Fabric? Color?" I asked. Cole's eyes twitched.

"Fabric…possibly something that is stiff but moveable," he said. I bit the inside of my cheek. "Color….gray," he finished. I watched his face. His eyes bore into mine but I could see there was a faraway look in them. He had no idea what he wanted. He was unprepared for this meeting. Either because he truly had no idea what he wanted or he was here for something else. I nodded.

"How about we do a charcoal gray suit, silver buttons and as for material, maybe wool," I said. I stared into his eyes. "Wool can feel light-weight. It's also durable. Which works for your job. And it has a bit of moisture-resistance," I said. His eyes regained focus and he cocked an eyebrow.

"Moisture resistance?" he questioned. I shrugged my shoulders.

"You know, water…blood," I said casually. His fingers twitched on his knee. I smiled.

"Your line of work is construction no? You must go on job sites. It's easy to get hurt," I said. Cole gave out a dry laugh. My heart was pounding in my chest. I had stayed up late researching whatever I could find on the Anders.

They owned a large construction company. The company mainly worked in their own city. But something told me they were looking to expand.

"Correct. Construction. May I ask a question?" he said.

"Of course," I said, closing my notebook.

"How long has your shop been here?" he asked. I tilted my head back and forth, taking my time to answer.

"I'm 28 so possibly 42 years," I said. I grew up in this shop. I knew the ins and outs even though I was unaware of the type of clientele we serviced. He nodded.

"You own the building?" he asked. I smirked.

"My grandfather does and one day it will be mine," I said, smiling.

"Ever think about selling?" he asked. I held onto my notebook.

"This shop is a part of my family, my blood. My family has poured their life into it. And one day it *will* be mine," I said. His eyes narrowed slightly. He laid back slightly in his chair, becoming comfortable.

"Everyone has a price," he said.

"Do the Anders plan on trying to buy my shop?" I asked, boldly. There it was. I needed to know if they were interested. If they were… well then I had a good idea about those men. Cole hesitated again. His eyes flashed with the same look from the charity ball. Regret. He cleared his throat.

"We are looking to expand. This area seems nice," he said, calmly. I was correct. I crossed my arms. This conversation was heading towards a cliff, but I'd be damned if I was going to get pushed over.

"This area is nice. People here are kind, respectful, and *loyal*. They love this shop as much as I do," I began. I looked around the shop, making eye contact with the cameras I could see. "They won't simply accept a newcomer who thinks they can run this town. There are other locations you can try to look into but this is mine," I said firmly.

A tick worked in Cole's jaw. He leaned his hands on his knees, staring at me. He wanted me to break. I could tell. My heart slowed. I had control over this conversation. He was in my shop. My area. Mine.

"I think you mean your grandfather," he commented. I uncrossed my legs.

"It belongs to the Silva family and I'm a Silva," I said. He glanced around again.

"Is your grandfather around? I missed him at the charity ball," he said, casually. My body tightened. I didn't like his tone. He wanted to see my grandfather but he got me instead. And now we were sitting here in a battle of words unspoken.

"He is not. But soon. Would you like a meeting?" I asked. He leaned back in his chair. The last thing I wanted was for my *avô* to be in the same room as Cole. He looked at me up and down.

"There are some things I would like to discuss with him," he said. I scoffed.

"And you think you can't discuss them with me?" I said. Another tick in his jaw. Cole opened his mouth to say something but I held up a hand. I stood up, enjoying looking down at him. "Mr. Anders, I will gladly make you a suit. As for my grandfather I can tell you for certain that he will not give up his shop to anyone. Especially The Anders family," I said. Cole stood up, near my height. He narrowed his eyes. But I wasn't going to let him scare me.

"But to the Costa's?" he asked. I clamped down on my tongue to keep my features schooled. The Costa's? My *avô* wouldn't think of handing our shop to them would he? He couldn't. This was ours. I rolled my shoulders back.

"To no one. Now are you still interested in a suit?" I asked.

After finalizing the suit that he legitimately wanted Cole walked out and I scurried to the office. My heart finally began racing as adrenaline coursed through my body. What the fuck was that?

So the Anders really wanted my territory. They think my *avô* would hand it over to the Costa's. I sat in my *avô's* chair and stared at my reflection on the computer screen. I hadn't known about the mafia for long but one thing I knew was that the Silva family and this shop was important to the Loba Vista community and I'd be damned if I let any man take it from me.

CHAPTER 13

Family Dinner

WHISKEY IS A GREAT WAY TO LOOSEN UP THE LIPS OF LYING MEN

I found myself back at the Costa's for dinner. The old man was in fact Dante's father. I could see the resemblance. Same inky black hair that was peppered with streaks of white and gray eyes.

He sat at the head while Luca and Dante flanked his sides. I decided to take the head at the other end. There was an empty seat across from me.

"Thank you for inviting me to dinner Mr. Costa," I said politely. Dante's father smiled at me.

"Please call me Michael," he said. I nodded. A throat cleared behind me. I turned around to see my *avô*. A smile broke across my face.

"*Avô!*" I said. I stood up and walked over to give him a big hug. My body curled over his. My *avô* laughed.

"You're going to break my rib, *querida*. I wasn't gone that long," he teased. I pulled away, glaring. He ignored my look, patted my back and headed back to the table. The men stood up to greet my *avô* with hugs and handshakes. I took my seat quietly.

"Lucia?" my *avô* asked. I looked at him. He eyed me and then the seat. In retrospect now that my *avô* arrived he should have taken the end of the table seat.

But he's been gone and I've had to deal with his shit so I deserved this seat. I pointed to the empty seat across from me. He said nothing taking his seat but tension hung tightly in the air.

"Should we discuss what I have to say before or after dinner?" I asked, crossing my arms. Michael chuckled.

"She's a lot like Anna," Michael commented, mentioning my *avó*. I smiled at the compliment. My *avô* snorted.

"You have no idea," my *avô* said, shaking his head.

"After dinner, Lucia," Dante said. He must have noticed my impatience. I nodded.

"Let's eat, boys," I commanded.

HALF AN HOUR later we were back in the meeting room where Dante made a mess of me on the table. I glanced at it before looking at Dante. He smirked against his whiskey glass. I rolled my eyes. At the table Michael sat at the head and we sat around.

"It's good to see you Michael," my *avô* said. They cheered their glasses.

"I wish it was under better circumstances Diogo," Michael said. I watched the men, analyzing their relaxed bodies, watching as they spoke to each other casually. Luca sat next to me and squeezed my knee. I shot him a small smile before taking a sip of whiskey. My *avô* looked at me, his eyes disappearing into sadness.

"I guess now it is time," he said. I nodded.

"May I start?" I asked. The men nodded and I took a deep breath before explaining what happened with Cole. "From my understanding and assumption of the situation the Anders want a way to take our shop, or should I say our territory," I said, glancing at my *avô*. "They were looking for papers of some kind when their men broke in. And yes it was their men. Cole made it obvious by our conversation. So now this is the part where you tell me that this neural territory is bullshit," I said. Everyone remained quiet. My *avô* sighed deeply.

"*Tambem, querida.* It's true to an extent. Back then there was a war between us and the Americans. We pushed them back to where they are now. We all agreed on the territories. But then your parents died and your *avó* was killed," my *avô* began. My stomach sank. Killed? By who?

"It was just you and I. I swore that I would protect you from this life. So I disbanded the Portuguese mafia and entered an agreement with the Costa's," he continued. I knew it. Michael nodded. I took a deep breath, processing it all. "We declared that our territory would be neutral. The others accepted. Although the Costa's are the ones who run things in our city ," he continued.

"The Americans are no longer accepting of this agreement and want to take it. They must be searching for the contract we made," my *avô* finished explaining.

"Pause, is this agreement a secret from the other clans?" I asked.

"It is. All the clans agreed on the neutrality portion but no one knows that we've been watching over Loba Vista," Dante said.

"So you're telling me that our territory is owned by the Italians?" I said, anger seeping into my voice. I really liked Dante and Luca. Hell, even Michael was cool but I didn't like the idea of them owning something that used to be ours. My *avô* nodded. "And now the Americans want to take back what is rightfully mine?" I asked. My *avô's* eyes sparkled.

"Yours?" Michael asked. I stared at him before taking another sip of whiskey. I enjoyed the burn and I used it to fuel my anger.

"Yes. The shop belongs to the Silva's," I said. My *avô* tapped his fingers on the table.

"And the city?" Michael asked.

"It *was* ours and was supposed to keep being ours," I pointed out.

"That may be so but the land is no longer ours. It's the Costa's," my *avô* pointed out. "The Anders are their problem now," he said. I scoffed.

"The Anders are everyone's problem. They believe the territory is still ours because this agreement you have is a secret. Cole made that clear when he asked about whether or not I would give the shop to the Costa's," I said. "Which by the way I made it known that was a no. Imagine what the other mafias will think once they find out just how much land the Costa's own. It won't be good. You'll have more than the Anders to worry about," I said. Dante sighed.

"She's right. Anders won't be the only ones wanting war," Dante said. I glanced at him, surprised he agreed with me.

"The Anders are working on something. They came into *your* shop. They spoke to Lucia. Who can I say stood her ground," Luca pointed out. I gave him a small smile. Michael and my *avô* glanced at each other.

"What do you want, Lucia?" Michael asked. I stared, taken aback by the question. What did I want? I wanted to avoid a war. I wanted our land to be rightfully ours. I wanted to work in peace at my shop.

"For you to rip that agreement," I said.

"Lucia!" my *avô* exclaimed. "The Costa's have been fair with us throughout these years. They've protected us."

"Everyone still thinks it's a part of our territory. You giving it back won't ruffle any feathers," I said. "It won't cause anything," I corrected myself for him to understand. My *avô* stood up and Michael waved at him to sit down.

"There's more," Michael said, motioning for me to continue. He watched me carefully. I took a deep breath, choosing my words carefully.

"The Anders haven't seen the Portuguese mafia in years. That's why they thought it was so easy to break into our shop. *That's* why they thought it was so easy to speak to me. The next time they won't be as kind. I'm suggesting we rebuild the Portuguese mafia and continue working with you guys to ensure the Americans stay in their little corner," I said. Michael rocked his head back and forth in debate. My *avô* stared at me, a mix of shock, worry and amazement.

"She is very much like Anna," Michael commented with a smile.

"I knew this attitude of yours would come back to annoy me," my *avô* said. I looked at Dante and Luca who offered me proud smiles.

"In all honesty I think you're correct Lucia. If word were to get out that we had control of the Silva territory it would signal to the other clans of a possible war. Men become greedy when they see others that have more," Michael said, leaning back in his chair. "I would rather have word get out that the Silva clan is back in full force. The Anders have some-thing planned," he said. I nodded.

"You're right as always *querida*," my *avô* said, placing a hand on top of mine. My body hummed at the praise. This was going swimmingly.

"One condition," Michael said. I swallowed as I stared into his steel gray eyes. Well I thought it was going swimmingly.

"The Portuguese mafia needs a leader," Michael said. I stared at him in confusion.

"My *avô* is back," I said. My *avô* chuckled. I stared at the men.

"The Silva family has never been a patriarchy," my *avô* said. My heart banged against my chest. There was no way he was suggesting what I thought he was suggesting. "I didn't run the clan, *meu amor*. Your *avó* did," he said. My jaw dropped. I pulled my hand back.

"There's no way I could be in charge," I said. Dante scoffed. I felt Luca's hand on my shoulder.

"Do you not remember putting our men in their place?" Luca said. My *avô* raised an eyebrow in surprise. "In front of Dante and Michael?" he added.

"She's a natural leader," Dante said. Michael nodded in agreement. I shook my head. There was no way I could do that.

"What men will follow a woman's orders?" I asked. Sure I handled Dante's men but that didn't mean they were happy about it. They looked ready to kill. The only reason they didn't was because of Dante.

"My men will follow you," Dante said. "I'll make them," he stated.

"Or else," Luca said. I looked at my *avô*. Could I do this? Could I lead a group of men? But wasn't this my legacy? I would only be taking back what was rightfully mine.

"I knew one day this would happen. You always held the same fire as your *avó*. You can do this if you choose but you don't have to," my *avô* said. For some reason his last line left a bad taste in my mouth.

If I let the Costa family continue to have control then that would mean giving up what my grandparents had built. I would be letting what my *avô* had started disappear into the wind. They built Loba Vista. They took care of it. And now our name no longer carried weight. We were *just* a seamstress shop.

Someone murdered my *avô*. Someone forced us to retreat into hiding.

But I had the strength and power to bring us back. I took a deep breath before meeting Michael's eyes.

"Burn the agreement. The Silva's are back."

CHAPTER 14

Family Secrets Revealed

THE TRUTH CAN GIVE YOU POWER IF YOU WIELD IT RIGHT

Michael easily agreed to absolve the agreement my *avô* had made. I watched the papers burn in the fireplace. Turns out he had kept them safe.

A weight slowly began lifting off my shoulders. There was still so much to learn. I had to learn all about the mafia clans and how they ran. I needed to learn which contacts I could still use. My thoughts drifted to Danny. I hoped he was someone I could still rely on. Most importantly I needed to learn the truth about my family history.

I glanced at Michael and my *avô*. They clinked their glasses together. Apparently those two had been best friends since they were in their 20s navigating America together. They each brought up their respective clans from the ground up. They were each other's best man. When my parents were killed in a car accident it was the Costa family that made sure my family was okay.

"I'm so sorry Lucia," my *avô* said once the other men had left the room. I nodded quietly.

"Honestly everything makes sense now. The secretive clients and times where I needed to be out of the room, out of the shop," I said. He nodded along. "So *avô* was in charge?" I asked tentatively. He gave a whisper of a smile.

"She was. She led with a powerful fist and a soft heart. It was amazing to watch her. She knew when to draw the line and when to draw blood. She kept a balance that was well respected," he said, lost in the past. I nodded. From my faint memories of her that seemed about right.

"So they were murdered?" I asked. Because I had been so young when everything happened I almost felt detached. I knew my parents loved me. I remember warm hugs and gentle forehead kisses. But that's where it ended.

"With your parents we believe that it may have been just a simple car accident. But a few weeks later your *avó* was shot. Sniper. She was meeting the Korean clan about a partnership," he said. My brows furrowed. A partnership? That was interesting.

"The Koreans weren't behind it?" I asked. My *avô* shook his head.

"*Senhora* Kim almost lost her life when it happened. She-she tried to keep Anna alive," my *avô* said, staring into his whiskey glass. "Instead of looking more into who the sniper was I had us going into hiding. Nothing happened once the Costa's started patrolling our area and no one questioned it," he said. I nodded. Given his relationship with Michael that made sense. He was a man grieving the loss of his family.

"They might when they see we're back," I said. The Portuguese mafia has remained quiet for the past 23 years. I'm breaking that silence," I said. He nodded, taking a deep breath.

"It won't be easy *querida*. First we have to gather the people. Show that we're back and that *you* are in charge. You have to be strong. While this is in your blood you've had your eyes closed to it all," he said. I let out a breath.

I was going to be witnessing things I had only seen in movies and read in books. Those things were going to be a daily reality. It wouldn't matter how much I mentally prepared, it was going to be a lot.

"That's why I have you and the Costa's with me, to support me," I said. My *avô* smiled.

"It seems like my little *coelhinha* is becoming a *loba*," he said. I smiled, reaching for a hug.

"She always was, *avô*."

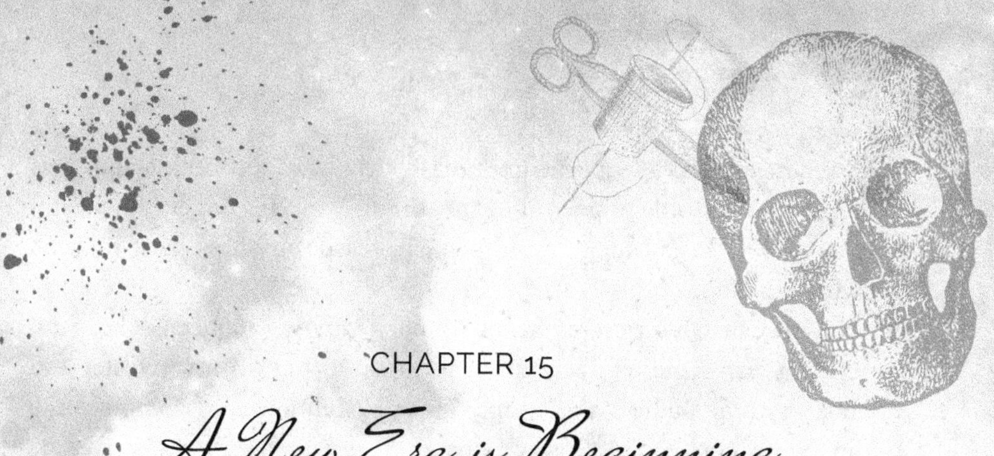

CHAPTER 15

A New Era is Beginning

A CROWN WILL ALWAYS BE THE BEST ACCESSORY

My *avô* and I agreed to stay the night at the Costa's. It was late and he was still jet lagged. I walked my *avô* back to the room he was staying in before heading to the living room. The stars twinkled behind the window. I heard shuffling behind me and turned to see Dante shirtless. He waved for me to follow and I did. We ended up at his room.

He had a massive room with an ensuite bathroom and a king size bed covered in black sheets. I snorted. Of course the dark brooding mafia man had black sheets. I felt his hands on my shoulders.

He began massaging and a low moan slipped out of me. He pressed his lips to my neck, tugging down my turtleneck. I had worn it to hide the hickeys that he and Luca left.

I leaned away offering more of myself. His lips made my body buzz alive as he left wet kisses. His hands dragged down my back, before slipping under my sweater. His thumbs pressed into my lower back, releasing tension I hadn't known were there.

"How are you, *Bella*?" he asked. I stared at the bed. I wasn't sure. I didn't feel scared or anything, surprisingly. Instead everything felt right. I felt powerful.

"I think I'm okay. This feels right for some reason," I whispered. His hands came around to squeeze my breasts. My head fell back against his shoulder as his hands slipped underneath my bra. His fingers found my nipples and he began tugging on them. I pressed my hips back into his growing erection.

"It's because you were meant to be a *donna*, a queen," he said, against my ear. I pulled away from his grasp to tug off my sweater and unhook my bra. Dante stared at me, his eyes lighting up. I could see the outline of his cock against his sweatpants.

Next I removed my pants, leaving myself in a pair of burgundy lace panties. I sat on his bed, opening my legs to him. In understanding Dante knelt down, his hands on my thighs. He placed kisses against the tender skin of the inside of my thighs. I shuddered at the feeling. My hands ran through his dark hair.

"I'm a queen?" I asked, breathless. He nodded, kissing up my stomach. I arched my back, needing more. He pushed me back, crawling on top. He lowered his hips and I gasped at the feel of his cock, rubbing against the panties. The lace created a delicious friction. I wrapped my legs around him, pulling him closer. He began sucking on my nipple, his teeth occasionally grazing it, teasing me, eliciting hushed whimpers from me. I pulled his face for a kiss.

I was hungry. I was desperate as I dug my heels into his lower back, my hands scratching his skin, pulling him closer. I needed to lose myself. His hand gripped my ass and he flipped us so I was on top. I yelped as he smacked my ass. His gray eyes darkened.

"You might be a queen, but tonight you're my whore," he whispered. I pulled up, grinding against him. His hands gripped my hips.

"Only if that means I win again," I said. My hands moved to play with my nipples. Dante groaned at the sight.

"I like to think you've been winning this entire time," he said, tugging at my panties. I lifted up enough to let him tear it off of me. He tossed them to the side and I smirked as he shoved his sweatpants down.

I rubbed myself against his cock. He bucked up, eyes shutting close. His hands ran up and down my body, before squeezing my ass. He gave me another sharp smack that sent me rocking faster against him.

"I like being greedy," I said in a gasp. I was so wet I was easily sliding back and forth on him. I leaned forward slightly, enjoying how his head teased my entrance. I could push back and let him slip in.

But not yet. I met his eyes again. He raised an eyebrow in question. I smirked, hopping off his dick and moving so my ass was in his face. I gripped his dick in my hand. Dante let out a strangled gasp. I looked over my shoulder, wiggling my ass in his face.

"Let's be greedy, shall we?" I said. Dante spread my cheeks apart as his mouth ghosted my entrance. His tongue gave a rough lick from my clit to my entrance and I nearly collapsed on his dick. "Fuck," I hissed.

He pressed me down onto his mouth. His tongue reached my clit and he sucked hard. Two could play at that. I gave his cock a rough lick, enjoying my taste on him. I swirled my tongue around his head and he bucked for me to take him deeper. I rocked against his mouth and bobbed up and down on his cock, sucking harder. His arm wrapped around waist, pulling me harder against him. I squeezed my hand, pumping up and down, in tangent with my mouth. I groaned. This was heavenly.

The pressure of his tongue shifted. He went from rough sucks to gentle licks. I could feel myself getting closer to the edge. I was beginning to lose focus. I began sucking his cock faster, enjoying how full he felt in my mouth. Dante pulled his mouth away for a second.

"Be my good little whore tonight *Bella*. Squeeze harder," he said, voice ragged. I did as I was told and Dante's fingers dug deeper into my ass.

He focused on my clit. He rolled his tongue as he sucked me, matching my pace and soon I felt the rush of the buildup. I squeezed his balls with my other hand. He groaned deeply.

An electricity seemed to spark from deep within and I began choking on his dick. The gagging must have turned him on because Dante became relentless as we chased each other's orgasms.

His body tightened beneath mine and he exploded in my mouth. He shoved two fingers inside and curled them. I quickly swallowed, feeling myself falling over the edge as my orgasm slammed into me. I bit down on his leg to muffle my screams.

"Fucking shit," I whispered as Dante pumped the last bit of my orgasm away. I pull away from him, collapsing on the bed. Dante chuckled darkly.

"I like being greedy with you," he whispered, as he kissed my ankle. I rolled off of him, catching my breath.

"Same, same," I managed to say. Dante lightly smacked my ass. I gasped feeling his finger play with my tight hole.

"We're going to have this eventually," he murmured, biting the back of my thigh. My face burned.

We. That was a promise.

I pushed him away to scurry to the bathroom. After relieving myself I came back to the bedroom to Dante holding up a robe for me. I smiled at him.

"Let's get some water," he said, wrapping an arm around me. I followed him back to the kitchen. It was massive with beige granite counters and brick backsplash. The stove was black with gold metal detailing and it reminded me of one of the old school European stoves. I could only imagine the amount of bread I could make.

He handed me a glass of water and we both stared out the window over the sink. We could see the city skyline. To the right was the Costa's. To the left was my territory. *Mine.*

I was in charge of all of those that dwelled in Loba Vista. It felt like a heavy burden. Or maybe it wasn't a burden. Maybe it was a chance to change things. I could make things better. I could make things right.

I heard footsteps behind me and saw a shirtless Luca walk in. A similar tattoo that Dante had on his forearm was on Luca's left shoulder. He glanced at both of us with a smirk. Luca's hair was messy and he had a tattoo of a lion on his chest.

"Hydration is important," Luca commented. I flushed and turned to look back out the window. Luca kissed my cheek, before taking my cup and taking a sip. "How do you feel?" he asked. I rolled my eyes.

"Right now I feel sated. Now about the meeting we had? Concerned," I answered truthfully. From the corner of my eyes Dante's lips twitched.

"How do you plan on reinstating the Portuguese mafia?" Dante asked. I leaned heavier against the counter, enjoying the warmth of both men.

"You have to let your people know the Silva Family is back in business," Luca said. I nodded in agreement. I've had different ideas run through my head since the meeting. There was one that stuck out the most. I saw myself smiling in the window's reflection.

"I'll do it the way every Portuguese woman does when they want to get something done," I said. I glanced at both men. "I'm going to host a feast. There's a soccer game coming up. Benfica versus Barcelona. I'm going to let the people know there's a Portuguese lunch happening and that a Silva is hosting it," I said. Dante smiled at me and placed a kiss on my neck. I felt Luca's hand slide down my back to squeeze my hip. My heart rattled against my chest.

"The Anders think they can have what's mine," I said.

"We'll help you," Dante said, against my neck. My eyes flickered to Luca who smiled. His blue eyes sparkled. He pressed himself flush against my side.

"In whatever way you need," Luca whispered as he placed a kiss on my temple. I looked back out the window. Both men were wrapped around me.

Not only did I have them but I had their men. I had the entire Costa's clan wrapped around my finger. They were a string that was going to help me sew my clan back together. The web I had begun to stitch was growing. The Silva's were back and we were going to fight to keep our territory no matter what.

"It's time for everyone to know that this princess is taking her crown," I said.

The end...for now

Acknowledgments

We're honestly going to keep this short and sweet. Who do I have to thank? Well TikTok. I randomly was sewing a dress, turned on the camera and started to make up a plot on the spot. That quick video turned into 80 parts and everyone wanting a book. So I finally did it after three years. For anyone who has been wanting this story, thank you for pushing me to make it happen.

For the special person who had a great time sharing those videos with her friend I know she would have enjoyed this.

Also thank you to my friends Jennette, Ime, Michelle, Kaylea, Ash and Miguel who have also been wanting this story.

Special thanks to Ruby whose writing sprints got me to finish this. I enjoy our endless yelling and screenshots of spicy scenes. It's been an honor to also be a part of your writing journey. Is it too soon to ask that we continue this writing buddy romance forever? Also everyone read Snap Shot if you want a hot golden retriever hockey player and a snarky Desi lady lawyer. You'll be hot AND cry.

Lastly, I hope this story lived up to what you expected…and if it didn't well there's other books you can read.

About the Author

Isabel Catrina is a dark-ish romance author. Emphasis on dark-ish because she isn't sure how far she'll take any story but at the end of the day she wants to be able to sleep at night with the thoughts in her head.

You can follow her on Instagram/TikTok:
@authorisabelcatrina
You can receive her newsletter on substack:
A Bookworm's Diary by Isabel Barreiro

You can also check out her cozy paranormal small town series under the name Isabel Barreiro.

<u>Falling For Fairy Tales</u>
Childhood friends to lovers | Workplace romance | Paranormal small town | Magical cocktails | Slow burn
<u>Lust, Love & Pixie Dust</u>
Friends-ish with benefits | No kissing curse | Paranormal small town | Fast Burn | Waterfall shenanigans

www.ingramcontent.com/pod-product-compliance
Lightning Source LLC
Chambersburg PA
CBHW071756150726
47998CB00005B/1958